OF PEOPLE
AND PUPPETS

"*On the one hand, as you're aware,*" said Ti to Telzey, "*I'm trying to see how close I can come to turning a Martri puppet into a fully functioning human being.* On the other hand, I'm trying to complete the process of turning a human being into a Martri puppet, or into an entity that is indistinguishable from one. The same thing, of course, could be attempted at less highly evolved life levels. But using the human species is more interesting and has definite advantages—quite aside from the one that it's around in abundance, so there's no problem of picking up as much research material as I need or of the type I happen to want."

Telzey said, "And after you've done it—after you've proved you can turn people into puppets and puppets into people—what are you going to do?"

Ti patted her shoulder. "That, my dear, needn't concern you at present. However, I do have some very interesting plans."

The
TELZEY TOY

by
James H. Schmitz

DAW BOOKS, INC.
DONALD A. WOLLHEIM, PUBLISHER

1301 Avenue of the Americas
New York, N. Y.   10019

FIRST PRINTING, DECEMBER 1973

1 2 3 4 5 6 7 8 9

PRINTED IN U.S.A.

The Telzey Toy

An auburn-haired, petal-cheeked young woman who belonged in another reality came walking with feline grace along a restaurant terrace in Orado City where Telzey had stopped for lunch during a shopping excursion.

Telzey watched her approach. This, she decided, was quite strange. Going by her appearance and way of moving, the woman seemed to be someone she'd met before. But she knew they hadn't met before. She knew also, in a curiously definite manner, that the woman simply couldn't be on this terrace in Orado City. She existed in other dimensions, not here, not now.

The woman who didn't exist here glanced at Telzey in passing. There was no recognition in the look. Telzey shifted her chair slightly, watched the familiar-unfamiliar phantom take another table not far away, pick up an order disk. A very good-looking young woman with a smooth unsmiling face, fashionably and expensively dressed—and nobody else around seemed to find anything at all unreasonable in her presence.

So perhaps, Telzey reflected, it was her psi senses that found it unreasonable. She slipped out a thought probe, held it a moment. It produced no telepathic touch response, no suggestion of shielding. If the woman was psi, she was an atypical variety. She'd taken a snack glass from the table dispenser by now, was sipping at it—

Comprehension came suddenly. No mystery after all, Telzey told herself, half amused, half disappointed. A year ago, she'd gone with some acquaintances to take in a Martridrama. The woman looked and walked exactly like one of the puppets they'd seen that evening, one who played a minor role but appeared enough of an individual to have left an impression in memory. No wonder it had seemed a slightly uncanny encounter—Martri puppets didn't go strolling around the city by themselves.

Another thought drifted up then, quite idly.

Or did they?

Telzey studied the pale profile again. Her skin began prickling. It was a most improper notion, but there might be a quick way of checking it. Some minds could be tapped easily, some with varying degrees of difficulty, some not at all. If this woman happened to be one of the easy ones, a few minutes of probing could establish what she was—or wasn't.

It took longer than that. Telzey had contact presently, but it remained tenuous and indistinct; she lost it repeatedly. Then, as she reestablished it again, a little more definitely now, the woman finished her snack drink and stood up. Telzey slipped a pay chit for her lunch into the table's receptacle, waited till her quarry turned away, then followed her toward a terrace exit.

A Martri puppet was a biological organism superficially indistinguishable from a human being. It had a brain which could be programmed, and which responded to cues with human speech and human behavior. Whether something resembling the human mind could be associated with that kind of brain was a point Telzey hadn't found occasion to consider before. She was no Martriphile, didn't, in fact, particularly care for that form of entertainment.

There was mind here, and the blurred patterns she'd touched seemed human. But she hadn't picked up enough to say it couldn't be the mind of a Martri puppet. . . .

The woman took an airtaxi on another terrace of the shopping complex. As it rose from the platform, Telzey got into the next taxi in line and told the driver to follow the one that had just left. The driver spun his colleague's car into his screen.

"Don't know if I can," he said then. "He's heading up into heavy traffic."

Telzey smiled at him. "Double fare for trying!"

They set off promptly in pursuit. Telzey clung to her contact, began assembling additional data. Some minutes later, the driver announced, "Looks like we've lost them!"

She already knew it. Distance wasn't necessarily a factor in developing mind contact. In this case it had been a factor. The crosstown traffic stream was dense, close to the automatic reroute point. The impressions she'd been receiving, weak at best, had begun to be flooded out increasingly by intruding impressions from other minds. The car they'd been pursuing must be several miles away by now. She let contact fade, told the driver to return to the shopping complex, and settled back very thoughtfully in her seat.

Few Martriphiles saw anything objectionable in having puppets killed literally on stage when a drama called for it. It was an essential part of Martri realism. The puppets were biological machines; the emotions and reactions they displayed were programmed ones. They had no self-awareness—that was the theory.

What she'd found in the mind of the auburn-haired woman seemed less important than what she hadn't found there, though she'd been specifically searching for it.

That woman knew where she was, what she was doing. There'd been scraps of recent memory, some moment-to-moment observations, an intimation of underlying purpose. But she appeared to have no personal sense of herself. She knew she existed—an objective fact among other facts, with no more significance than the others.

In other words, she did seem to lack self-awareness. As far as Telzey had been able to make out, the term had no meaning for her. But the contact hadn't been solid enough or extensive enough to prove it.

On the face of it, Telzey was telling herself an hour later, the thing was preposterous. She'd had a wild notion, had tried to disprove it and failed. She'd even turned up some evidence which might seem to favor the notion. It remained wild. Why waste more time on the matter?

She bit her thumb irritably, dialed an information center for data on Martridramas and Martri puppets, went over the material when it arrived. There wasn't much there she didn't already know in a general way. A Martri stage was a programmed computer which in turn programmed the puppets, and directed them during a play under the general guidance of the dramateer. While a play was new, no two renditions of it were exactly the same. Computer and puppets retained some choice of action, directed always toward greater consistency, logic, and effect. Only when further inprovement was no longer possible did a Martridrama remain frozen and glittering—a thing become perfect of its kind. It explained the continuing devotion of Martriphiles.

It didn't suggest that such a thing as a runaway puppet was a possibility.

The Martri unit which had put on the play she had seen was no longer on Orado. She could find out where it was at present, but there should be simpler ways of determining what she wanted to know immediately. A name had turned up repeatedly in her study of the Martri material . . . Wakote Ti. He was locally available. A big man. Multilevel scientist, industrial tycoon, millionaire, philanthropist, philosopher, artist, and art collector. Above all, a Martri specialist of specialists. Wakote Ti designed, grew, and merchandised the finest puppets in the Hub, built and programmed the most advanced Martri stages, had written over fifty of the most popular plays, and was a noted amateur dramateer.

A Martriphile relative of one of Telzey's friends turned out to be an admirer and business associate of Wakote Ti. He agreed to let Telzey know the next time the great man appeared at his laboratories in Draise, and to arrange for an interview with him.

"The legality of killing a puppet is regarded as unarguable," said Wakote Ti.

A college paper she'd be preparing on the legal niceties involved in the practice had been Telzey's ostensible reason for requesting the interview.

He shrugged. "But I simply couldn't bring myself to do it! They have life and a mentality, however limited and artificial they may be. Most importantly, they have personality, character. It's been programmed into them, of course, but, to my feeling, the distinction between puppets and humanity is one of degree rather than kind. They're unfinished people. They act always in accordance with their character, not necessarily in accordance with the wishes of the composer or dramateer. I've been surprised many times by the twists they've given the roles I assigned to them. Always valid ones! They can't be forced to deviate from what they are. In that respect they seem more honest than many of us."

Ti gave Telzey an engaging smile. He was a large, strongly muscled man, middle-aged, with a ruddy complexion and grizzled black hair. There was an air of controlled energy about him; and boundless energy he must have, to accomplish as much as he did. There was also an odd gentleness in gesture and voice. It was very easy to like Ti.

And he had a mind that couldn't be touched by a telepath. Telzey had known that after the first few minutes—probe-immune. Too bad! She'd sooner have drawn the information she wanted from him without giving him any inkling of what she was after.

"Do you use real people as models for them?" she asked. "I mean when they're being designed."

"Physically?"

"Yes."

Ti shook his head. "Not any one person. Many. They're ideal types."

Telzey hesitated, said, "I had an odd experience a while ago. I saw a woman who looked so exactly like a Martri puppet I'd seen in a play, I almost convinced myself it was the puppet who'd somehow walked off the stage and got lost in the world outside. I suppose that would be impossible?"

Ti laughed. "Oh, quite!"

"What makes it impossible?"

"Their limitations. A puppet can be programmed to perform satisfactorily in somewhere between twenty and thirty-five plays. One of ours, which is currently in commercial use, can handle forty-two roles of average complexity. I believe that's the record.

"At best, that's a very limited number of specific situations as compared with the endlessly shifting variety of situations in the real world. If a puppet were turned loose there, the input stream would very quickly overwhelm its response capacity, and it would simply stop operating."

"Theoretically," said Telzey, "couldn't the response capacity be pushed up to the point where a puppet could act like a person?"

"I can't say it's theoretically impossible," Ti said. "But it would require a new technology." He smiled. "And since there are quite enough real people around, there wouldn't be much point to it, would there?"

She shook her head. "Perhaps not."

"We're constantly experimenting, of course." Ti stood up. "There are a number of advanced models in various stages of development in another part of the building. They aren't usually shown to visitors, but if you'd like to see them, I'll make an exception."

"I'd very much like to!" Telzey said.

She decided she wasn't really convinced. New technologies were being developed regularly in other fields—why not in that of Martri puppetry? In any case, she might be able to settle the basic question now. She could try tapping the mind of one or the other of the advanced models he'd be showing her, and see how what she found compared with the patterns she'd traced in the mystery woman.

That plan was promptly discarded again. Ti had opened the door to a large office, and a big-boned young man sitting there at a desk looked up at her as they came in.

He was a telepath.

The chance meeting of two telepathic psis normally followed a standard etiquette. If neither was interested in developing the encounter, they gave no sign of knowing the other was a psi. If one was interested, he produced a mental identification. If the other failed to respond, the matter was dropped.

Neither Telzey nor the young man identified themselves. Ti, however, introduced them. "This is Linden, my secretary and assistant," he said; and to Linden, "This is Telzey Amberdon, who's interested in our puppets. I'm letting her see what we have in the vaults at present."

Linden, who had come to his feet, bowed and said, "You'd like me to show Miss Amberdon around?"

"No, I'll do that," said Ti. "I'm telling you so you'll know where I am."

That killed the notion of probing one of the puppets in the vaults. Now they'd met, it was too likely that Linden would become aware of any telepathic activity in the vicinity. Until she knew more, she didn't want to give any hint of her real interest in the puppets. There were other approaches she could use.

The half hour she spent in the vaults with Ti was otherwise

informative. "This one," he said, "is part of an experiment designed to increase our production speed. Three weeks is still regarded as a quite respectable time in which to turn out a finished puppet. We've been able to do a good deal better than that for some while. With these models, starting from scratch and using new hypergrowth processes, we can produce a puppet programmed for fifteen plays in twenty-four hours." He beamed down at Telzey. "Of course, it's probably still faulty —it hasn't been fully tested yet. But we're on the way! Speed's sometimes important. Key puppets get damaged or destroyed, and most of some Martri unit's schedule may be held up until a replacement can be provided."

That night at her home in Orado City, Telzey had an uninvited visitor. She was half asleep when she sensed a cautious mental probe. It brought her instantly and completely awake, but she gave no immediate indication of having noticed anything. It mightn't be a deliberate intrusion.

However, it appeared then that it was quite deliberate. The other psi remained cautious. But the probing continued, a not too expert testing of the density of her screens, a search for a weakness in their patterns through which the mind behind them might be scanned or invaded.

Telzey decided presently she'd waited long enough. She loosened her screens abruptly, sent a psi bolt flashing back along the line of probe. It smacked into another screen. The probe vanished. Somebody somewhere probably had been knocked cold for an hour or so.

Telzey lay awake a while, reflecting. She'd had a momentary impression of the personality of the prowler. Linden? It might have been. If so, what had he been after?

No immediate answer to that.

2

There was a permanent Martri stage in Orado City, and Telzey had intended taking in a show there next day—a Martridrama looked like the best opportunity now to get in some discreet study on puppet minds. Her experience with the psi prowler made her decide on a shift in plans. If it had been Wakote Ti's secretary who'd tried to probe her, then it could be that Ti had some reason to be interested in a telepath who was interested in Martri puppets, and her activities might be coming under observation for a while. Hence she should make anything she did in connection with the puppets as difficult to observe as she could—which included keeping away from the Orado City stage.

She made some ComWeb inquiries, arrived presently by pop transport shuttle in a town across the continent, where a Martridrama was in progress. She'd changed shuttles several times on the way. There'd been nothing to indicate she was being followed.

She bought a ticket at the stage, started up a hall toward the auditorium entry—

She was lying on her back on a couch, in a large room filled with warm sunshine. There was no one else in the room.

Shock held her immobilized for a moment.

It wasn't only that she didn't know where she was, or how she'd got there. Something about *her* seemed different, changed, profoundly wrong.

Realization came abruptly—every trace of psi sense was gone. She tried to reach out mentally into her surroundings, and it was like opening her eyes and still seeing nothing. Panic began to surge up in her then. She lay quiet, holding it off, until her breathing steadied again. Then she sat up on the couch, took inventory of what she could see here. The upper two-thirds of one side of the room was a single great window open on the world outside. Tree crowns were visible beyond it. Behind the trees, a mountain peak reached toward a blue sky. The room was simply furnished with a long table of polished dark wood, some chairs, the low couch on which she sat. The floor was carpeted. Two closed doors were in the wall across from the window.

Her clothes—white shirt, white shorts, white stockings, and moccasins—weren't the ones she'd been wearing.

None of that told her much, but meanwhile the threat of panic had withdrawn. She swung around, slid her legs over the edge of the couch. As she stood up, one of the doors opened, and Telzey watched herself walk into the room.

It jolted her again, but less severely. Take another girl of a size and bone structure close enough to her own, and a facsimile skin, eye tints, a few other touches, could produce an apparent duplicate. There'd be differences, but too minor to be noticeable. She didn't detect any immediately. The girl was dressed exactly as she was, wore her hair as she wore hers.

"Hello," Telzey said, as evenly as she could. "What's this game about?"

Her double came up, watching her soberly, stopped a few feet away. "What's the last thing you remember before you woke up here?" she asked.

Her voice, too? Quite close to it, at any rate.

Telzey said guardedly, "Something like a flash of white light inside my head."

The girl nodded. "In Sombedaln."

"In Sombedaln. I was in a hall, going toward a door."

"You were about thirty feet from that door," said her double. "And behind it was the Martri auditorium. . . . Those are the last things I remember, too. What about psi? Has it been wiped out?"

Telzey studied her a moment. "Who are you?" she asked.

The double shrugged. "I don't know. I feel I'm Telzey Amberdon. But if I weren't, I might still feel that."

"If you're Telzey, whom am I?" Telzey said.

"Let's sit down," the double said. "I've been awake half an hour, and I've been told a few things. They hit me pretty hard. They'll probably hit you pretty hard."

They sat down on the edge of the couch. The double went on. "There's no way we could prove right now that I'm the real Telzey. But there might be a way we can prove that you are, and I'm not."

"How?"

"Psi," said the double. "Telzey used it. I can't use it now. I can't touch it. Nothing happens. If you—"

"I can't either," Telzey said.

The double drew a sighing breath.

"Then we don't know," she said. "What I've been told is that one of us is Telzey and the other is a Martri copy who thinks she's Telzey. A puppet called Gaziel. It was grown during the last two days like other puppets are grown, but it was engineered to turn into an exact duplicate of Telzey as she is now. It has her memories. It has her personality. They were programmed into it. So it feels it's Telzey."

Telzey said, after some seconds, "Ti?"

"Yes. There's probably no one else around who could have done it."

"No, I guess not. Why did he do it?"

"He said he'd tell us that at lunch. He was still talking to me when he saw in a screen that you'd come awake, and sent me down here to tell you what had happened."

"So he's been watching?" Telzey said.

The double nodded. "He wanted to observe your reactions."

"As to which of you is Telzey," said Ti, "and which is Gaziel, that's something I don't intend to let you know for a while!" He smiled engagingly across the lunch table at them. "Theoretically, of course, it would be quite possible that you're both puppets and that the original Telzey is somebody else. However, we want to have some temporary way of identifying you two as individuals."

He pulled a ring from his finger, put both hands under the table level, brought them to view again as fists. "You," he said to Telzy, "will guess which hand is holding the ring. If you guess correctly, you'll be referred to as Telzey for the time being, and you," he added to the double, "as Gaziel. Agreed?"

They nodded. "Left," Telzey said.

"Left it is!" said Ti, beaming at her, as he opened his hand and revealed the ring. He put it back on his finger, inquired of Linden, who made a fourth at the table, "Do you think she might have cheated by using psi?"

Linden glowered, said nothing. Ti laughed. "Linden isn't fond of Telzey at present," he remarked. "Did you know you knocked him out for almost two hours when he tried to investigate your mind?"

"I thought that might have happened," said Gaziel.

"He'd like to make you pay for it," said Ti. "So watch yourselves, little dears, or I may tell him to go ahead. Now as to your future—Telzey's absence hasn't been discovered yet. When it is, a well-laid trail will lead off Orado somewhere else, and it will seem she's disappeared there under circumstances suggesting she's no longer alive. I intend, you see, to keep her indefinitely."

"Why?" Telzey asked.

"She noticed something," said Ti. "It wouldn't have seemed too important if Linden hadn't found out she was a telepath."

"Then that *was* your puppet I saw?" Gaziel said. She glanced over at Telzey, added, "That one of us—Telzey— saw."

"That *we* saw," Telzey said. "That will be simplest for now."

Ti smiled. "You live up to my expectations! . . . Yes, it was my puppet. We needn't go further into that matter at present. As a telepath and with her curiosities aroused, Telzey might have become a serious problem, and I decided at once to collect her rather than follow the simpler route of having her eliminated. I had her background checked out, which confirmed the favorable opinions I'd formed during our discussion. She should make a most satisfactory subject. Within the past hour, she's revealed another very valuable quality."

"What's that?" Telzey said.

"Stability," Ti told her. "For some time, I've been interested in psis in my work, and with Linden's help I've been able to secure several of them before this." He shook his head. "They were generally poor material. Some couldn't even sustain the effect of realizing I had created an exact duplicate of them. They collapsed into uselessness. So, of course, did the duplicates. But look at you two! You adjusted immediately to the situation, have eaten with every indication of a good appetite, and are no doubt already preparing schemes to get away from old Ti."

Telzey said, "Just what is the situation? What are you planning to do with us?"

Ti smiled at her. "That will develop presently. There's no hurry about it."

"Another question," said Gaziel. "What difference does it make that Telzey's a psi when you've knocked out her psi ability?"

"Oh, that's not an irreversible condition," Ti informed her. "The ability will return. It's necessary to keep it repressed until I've learned how to harness it, so to speak."

"It will show up in the duplicate, too, not just in the original?" Gaziel asked.

Ti gave her an approving look. "Precisely one of the points I wish to establish! My puppets go out on various errands for me. Consider how valuable puppet agents with Telzey's psi talent could be—a rather formidable talent, as Linden here can attest!"

He pushed himself back from the table. "I've enjoyed your questions, but I have work to take care of now. For the moment, this must be enough. Stroll about and look over your new surroundings. You're on my private island. Two-thirds of it is an almost untouched wilderness. The remaining third is a cultivated estate, walled off from the forest beyond. You're restricted to the estate. If you tried to escape into the forest, you'd be recaptured. There are penalties for disobedience, but more importantly, the forest is the habitat of puppet extravaganzas—experimental fancies you wouldn't care to encounter! You're free to go where you like on the estate. The places I wouldn't wish you to investigate at present are outside your reach."

"They have some way of knowing which of us is which, of course," Gaziel remarked from behind Telzey. They were threading their way through tall flowering shrubbery on the estate grounds.

"It would be a waste of time trying to find out what it is, though," Telzey said.

Gaziel agreed. The Martri duplicate might be marked in a number of ways detectable by instruments but not by human senses. "Would it disturb you very much if it turned out you weren't the original?" she said.

Telzey glanced back at her. "I'm sure it would," she said soberly. "You?"

Gaziel nodded. "I haven't thought about it too much, but it seems there's always been the feeling that I'm part of something that's been there a long, long time. It wouldn't be at all good to find out now that it was a false feeling—that I was only myself, with nothing behind me."

"And somebody who wasn't even there in any form a short while ago," Telzey added. "It couldn't help being disturbing! But that's what one of us is going to find out eventually. And, as Ti mentioned, we may both be duplicates. You know, our minds do seem to work identically—almost."

"Almost," said Gaziel. "They must have started becoming different minds as soon as we woke up. But it should be a while before the differences become too significant."

"That's something to remember," Telzey said.

They emerged from the flower thicket, saw the mountain again in the distance, looming above the trees. It rose at the far tip of the island, in the forest area. The cultivated estate seemed to cover a great deal of ground. When they'd started out from a side door of the round gleaming-white building which stood approximately at its center, they couldn't see to the ends of it anywhere because groups of trees blocked the view in all directions. But they could see the mountain and had started off toward it.

If they kept on toward it, they would reach the wall which bordered the estate.

"There's one thing," Telzey said. "We can't ever be sure here whether Ti or somebody else isn't listening to what we say."

Gaziel nodded. "We'll have to take a chance on that."

"Right," Telzey said. "We wouldn't get very far if we stuck to sign language or counting on thinking the same way about everything."

They came to the estate wall ten minutes later. It was a wall designed to discourage at first glance any notions of climbing over it. Made of the same gleaming material as the central building, its smooth unbroken surface stretched up a good thirty-five feet above the ground. It curved away out of sight behind trees in either direction; but none of the trees they saw stood within a hundred feet of the wall. They turned left along it. Either there was a gate somewhere, or aircars were used to reach the forest.

They came to a gateway presently. Faint vehicle tracks in the grass led up to it from various directions. It was closed by a slab set into the wall, which appeared to be a sliding door. They could find no indication of a lock or other mechanism.

"Might be operated from the house."

It might be. In any case, the gateway seemed to be in regular use. They sat down on the grass some distance away to wait. And they'd hardly settled themselves when the doorslab drew silently back into the wall. A small enclosed ground vehicle came through; and the slab sealed the gateway again. The vehicle moved on a few yards, stopped. They hadn't been able to see who was inside, but now a small door opened near the front end. Linden stepped out and started toward them, scowling. They got warily to their feet.

"What are you doing here?" he asked as he came up.

"Looking around generally like Ti told us to," said Gaziel.

"He didn't tell you to sit here watching the gate, did he?"

"No," Telzey said. "But he didn't say not to."

"Well, I'm telling you not to," Linden said. "Move on! Don't let me find you around here again."

They moved on. When they glanced back presently, the vehicle had disappeared.

"That man really doesn't like us," Gaziel remarked thoughtfully.

"No, he doesn't," Telzey said. "Let's climb a tree and have a look at the forest."

They picked a suitable tree, went up it until they were above the level of the wall and could see beyond it. A paved road wound away from the area of the gate toward the mountain. That part of the island seemed to be almost covered with a dense stand of tropical trees; but, as on this side, no trees grew very close to the wall. They noticed no signs of animal life except for a few small fliers. Nor of what might be Ti's experimental Martri life.

Telzey said, "The gate controls are probably inside the cars they use when they go out there."

"Uh-huh—and the car Linden was in was armored." Gaziel had turned to study the surrounding stretches of the estate from their vantage point. "Look over there!" she said.

Telzey looked. "Gardening squad," she said after a moment. "Maybe we can find out something from them."

3

A flotilla of sixteen flat machines was gliding about purposefully a few inches above the lawns among the trees. An operator sat on each, manipulating controls. Two men on foot spoke now and then into communicators, evidently directing the work.

Gaziel nodded. "Watch that one!"

They'd approached with some caution, keeping behind trees for the most part, and hadn't yet been observed. But now one of the machines was coming in directly from the side toward the tree behind which they stood. The operator should be able to see them, but he was paying them no attention.

They studied him in uneasy speculation. There was nothing wrong about his motions; it was his expression. The eyes shifted around, but everything else seemed limply dead. The jaw hung half open; the lips drooped; the cheeks sagged. The machine came up almost to the tree, turned at a right angle, started off on another course.

Telzey said softly, "The other operators seem to be in about the same condition—whatever it is. But the supervisors look all right. Let's see if they'll talk."

They stepped out from behind the tree, started toward the closer of the two men on foot. He caught sight of them, whistled to draw his companion's attention.

"Well," he said, grinning amiably as they came up. "Dr. Ti's new guest, aren't you?" His gaze shifted between them. "And, uh, twin. Which is the human one?"

The other man, a big broad-shouldered fellow, joined them. Telzey shrugged. "We don't know. They wouldn't say."

The men stared. "Can't you tell?" the big one demanded.

"No," said Gaziel "We both feel we're human." She added, "From what Dr. Ti told us, you mightn't be real people either and you wouldn't know it."

The two looked at each other and laughed.

19

"Not likely!" the big man said. "A wirehead doesn't have a bank account."

"You do? Outside?" Gaziel said.

"Uh-huh. A healthy one. My name's Remiol, by the way. The little runt's Eshan."

"We're Telzey and Gaziel," said Telzey. "And maybe you could make those bank accounts a lot healthier."

They looked at her, then shook their heads decidedly.

"We're not helping you get away, if that's what you mean," Remiol said. Eshan added, "There'd be no way of doing it if we wanted to. You kids just forget about that and settle down! This isn't a bad place if you keep out of trouble."

"You wouldn't have to help us get away exactly," Telzey said. "How often do you go to the mainland?"

There was a sudden momentary vagueness in their expressions which made her skin prickle.

"Well," Remiol said, frowning and speaking slowly as if he had some difficulty finding the words, "about as often as we feel like it, I'd say. I . . ." He hesitated, gave Eshan a puzzled look.

"You could take out a message," Gaziel said, watching him.

"Forget it!" said Eshan, who seemed unaware of anything unusual in Remiol's behavior. "We work for Dr. Ti. The pay's great and the life's easy. We aren't going to spoil that setup!"

"All right," Telzey said after a moment. "If you don't want to help us, maybe you won't mind telling us what the setup is."

"Wouldn't mind at all!" said Remiol, appearing to return abruptly to normal. He gave Telzey a friendly grin. "If Dr. Ti didn't want us to talk to you, we'd have been told. He's a good boss—you know where you are with him. Eshan, give the wireheads a food break and let's sit down with the girl."

They sat down in the grass together. Gaziel indicated the machine operators with a hand motion. "You call them wireheads. They aren't humans but a sort of Martri work robot?"

"Not work robots," Remiol said. "Dr. Ti doesn't bother with those. These are regular puppets—maybe defectives, or some experiment, or just drama puppets who've played a few roles too many. When they get like this, they don't last more'n a year—then back they go to the stuff they grow them from. Meanwhile they're still plenty good for this kind of work."

"Might be a few real humans among them," Eshan said reflectively, looking over at the operators. "After a while, you don't think about it much—they're all programmed anyway."

"How do real humans get to be in that kind of shape?" Gaziel said.

The men shrugged. "Some experiment again," said Remiol. "A lot of important research going on in the big building here."

Telzey said, "How did you know one of us was a wirehead?"

"One of the lab workers told us," said Eshan. "She said Dr. Ti was mighty happy with the results. Some of his other twinning projects hadn't turned out so well."

Remiol winked at Telzey. "This one turned out perfect!"

She smiled. "You ever been on the other side of the wall?"

They had. Evidently, it was as unhealthy as Ti had indicated to go there unless one was in one of the small fleet of armored and armed vehicles designed for the purpose. The only really safe place on the forest side was a small control fort on the slope of the mountain, and that came under occasional attack. Eshan and Remiol described some of the Martri creations they'd seen.

"Why does Dr. Ti keep them around?" Gaziel asked.

"Uses them sometimes in the Martridramas he puts on here," said Remiol.

"And wait till you've seen one of those!" said Eshan. "That's real excitement! You don't see shows like that anywhere else."

"Otherwise," Remiol said, speaking of the forest puppets, "I guess it's research again. I worried at first about one of them coming over the wall. But it's never happened."

"Well, well!" said Ti. "Having a friendly gossip?"

He'd come floating out of a grove of trees on a hoverdisk and stopped a few feet away, holding the guide rail in his large hands.

"Hope you don't mind, Doctor," Remiol said. He and Eshan had got to their feet as Ti approached.

Ti smiled. "Mind? Not in the least. I'm greatly pleased that the new members of our little community have begun to make acquaintances so quickly. However, now we'll all be getting back to work, eh? Telzey and Gaziel, you can stand up here with me and we'll return to the house together."

They stepped up on the disk beside him, and it swung gently around and floated away, while the gardening machines lifted from the ground and began to reform into their interrupted work patterns.

"Fine fellows, those two!" said Ti, beaming down at Gaziel and Telzey. "They don't believe in overexerting themselves, of course. But then that isn't necessary here, and I prefer a relaxed and agreeable atmosphere around me."

Telzey said, "I understand it's sometimes rather exciting, too."

Ti chuckled. "That provides the counterpoint—the mental and emotional stimulus of the Martridrama! I need both. I'm always at my best here on the island! A room has been prepared for you two. You'll be shown there, and I'll come then shortly to introduce you to some of the most interesting sections of our establishment."

The groundcar Linden had been operating stood near the side door Telzey and Gaziel had used when they left the building. The hoverdisk went gliding past it to the door which opened as they approached, and into the building. In the hall beyond, it settled to the floor. They stepped down from it.

"Why, Challis!" said Ti heartily, gazing past Telzey. "What a pleasant surprise to see you back!"

Telzey and Gaziel looked around. A pale slender woman with light blue hair was coming across the hall toward them.

"This is my dear wife," Ti told them. He was smiling, but it seemed to Telzey that his face had lost some of its ruddy color. "She's been absent from the island for some time. I didn't know she was returning. . . ." He turned to Challis as she came up. "These are two very promising recruits, Challis. You'll be interested in hearing about my plans for them."

Challis looked over at them with an expression which was neither friendly nor unfriendly. It might have been speculative. She had pale gray eyes and delicately beautiful features. She nodded slightly; and something stirred eerily in Telzey's mind.

Ti said, "I'll send someone to show you two to your room." He took Challis by the arm. "Come, my dear! I must hear what you've been doing."

He went off toward a door leading from the hall, Challis moving with supple ease beside him. As the door closed on the pair, Telzey glanced at Gaziel.

Gaziel said blandly, "You know, Ti's wife reminds me of someone. But I simply can't remember who it is."

So she's noticed it, too—the general similarity in appearance and motion between Challis and the auburn-haired puppet who'd come walking along the restaurant terrace in Orado City. . . .

A brisk elderly woman appeared a few minutes later. She led them to a sizable room two building levels above the hall, showed them what it contained, including a wardrobe filled with clothing made to their measurements, and departed after telling them to get dressed and wait here for Dr. Ti.

They selected other clothes, put them on. They were the sort of things Telzey might have bought for herself and evidently had been chosen with considerable care. They opened the door then and looked out. No one was in sight. They went quickly and quietly back downstairs to the entrance hall.

Linden's armored car still stood where they had seen it. There was no one in sight here either. They went over to the car. It took only a moment to establish that its two doors were locked, and that the locks were of the mechanical type.

They returned hurriedly to their room.

4

"Here," said Ti, "you see my current pool of human research material."

They were on an underground level of the central building, though the appearance of the area didn't suggest it. It was a large garden, enclosed by five-story building fronts. Above was a milky skylight. Approximately a hundred people were in sight in the garden and on the building galleries. Most of them were young adults. There were few children, fewer of the middle-aged, no oldsters at all. They were well-dressed, well-groomed; their faces were placid. They sat, stood, moved unhurriedly about, singly and in groups. Some talked; some were silent. The voices were low, the gestures leisurely.

"They're controlled by your Martri computer?" Telzey asked.

Ti nodded. "They've all been programmed, though to widely varying degrees. Since they're not being used at the moment, what you see is a random phase of the standard nonsleeping activity of each of them. But notice the group of five at the fountain! They've cued one another again into the identical discussion they've had possibly a thousand times before. We can vary the activity, of course, or reprogram a subject completely. I may put a few of them through their paces for you a little later."

"What's the purpose of doing this to them?" said Gaziel.

Ti said, "These are converging lines of study. On the one hand, as you're aware, I'm trying to see how close I can come to turning a Martri puppet into a fully functioning human being. On the other hand, I'm trying to complete the process of turning a human being into a Martri puppet, or into an entity that is indistinguishable from one. The same thing, of course, could be attempted at less highly evolved life levels. But using the human species is more interesting and has definite advantages—quite aside from the one that it's around in abundance, so there's no problem of picking up as much research material as I need, or the type I happen to want."

"Aren't you afraid of getting caught?" Gaziel said.

Ti smiled. "No. I'm quite careful. Every day, an amazing number of people in the Hub disappear, for many reasons. My private depredations don't affect the overall statistics."

Telzey said, "And after you've done it—after you've proved you can turn people into puppets and puppets into people—what are you going to do?"

Ti patted her shoulder. "That, my dear, needn't concern you at present. However, I do have some very interesting plans."

Gaziel looked up at him. "Is this where the one of us who's the original Telzey will go?"

"No," Ti said. "By no means. To consign her to the research pool would be inexcusably wasteful. Telzey, if matters work out satisfactorily, will become my assistant."

"In what way?"

"That woman puppet you were so curious about—you tried to investigate its mind, didn't you?"

Gaziel hesitated an instant. "Yes."

"What did you find?"

"Not too much. It got away from me too quickly. But it seemed to me that it had no sense of personal existence. It was there. But it was a nothing that did things."

"Did you learn what it was doing?"

"No."

Ti rubbed his jaw. "I'm not sure I believe that," he remarked thoughtfully. "But it makes no difference now. I have a number of such puppet agents. Obviously, a puppet which is to be employed in that manner should never be developed from one of the types that are in public dramatic use. That it happened in this case was a serious error; and the error was Linden's. I was very much annoyed with him. However, your ability to look into its mind is a demonstration of Telzey's potential value. Linden, as far as I can judge the matter, is a fairly capable telepath. But puppet minds are an almost complete blur to him, and when it comes to investigating human minds in the minute detail I would often prefer, he hasn't been too satisfactory. Aside from that, of course, he has many other time-absorbing duties.

"We already know that Telzey is a more capable telepath than Linden in at least two respects. When her psi functions have been restored, she should become extremely useful." Ti waved his hand about. "Consider these people! The degree of individual awareness they retain varies, depending on the extent and depth of the programming they've undergone. In some, it's not difficult to discern. In others, it's become almost impossible by present methods. That would be one of Telzey's tasks. She should find the work interesting enough."

"She'll be a wirehead?" Telzey said.

"Oh, yes, you'll both be programmed," Ti told her. "I could hardly count on your full collaboration otherwise, could I? But it'll be delicate work. Our previous experiments have indicated that programming psi minds presents special difficulties in any case, and I want to be quite sure that nothing goes wrong here. Your self-awareness shouldn't be affected for one thing." He smiled. "I believe I've come close to solving those problems. We'll see presently."

Telzey said, "What do you have in mind for the one who isn't Telzey?"

"Ah! Gaziel!" Ti's eyes sparkled. "I'm fascinated by the possibilities there. The question is whether our duplication processes have brought on the duplication of the original psi potential. There was no way of testing indirectly for that, but we should soon know. If they have, Gaziel will have become the first Martri psi. In any case, my dears, you can rest assured, whichever you may be, that each of you is as valued by me as the other and will be as carefully handled. I realize that you aren't reconciled to the situation, but that will come in time."

Telzey looked at him. Part lies, part truth. He'd handle them carefully, all right. Very carefully. They had value. And he'd weave, if they couldn't prevent it, a tightening net of compulsions about them they'd never escape undestroyed. What self-awareness they'd have left finally might be on the level of that of his gardening supervisors. . . .

"Eshan and Remiol are wireheads, too, aren't they?" she said.

Ti nodded. "Aside from Linden and myself and at present you two, everyone on the island is—to use that loose expression—a wirehead. I have over a hundred and fifty human employees here, and, like the two with whom you spoke, they're all loyal, contented people."

"But they don't have big bank accounts outside and aren't allowed off the island by themselves?" Telzey said.

Ti's eyebrows lifted.

"Certainly not!" he said. "Those are pleasant illusions they maintain. There are too many sharp inquiring minds out there to risk arrangements like that. Besides, while I have a great deal of money, I also have a great many uses for it. Why should I go to unnecessary expense?"

"We didn't really think you had," Gaziel said.

"And now," said Ti, stopping before a small door, "you are about to enjoy a privilege granted to none other of our employees! Behind this door is the brain and nerve center of Ti's Island—the Dramateer Room of the Martri computer." He took out two keys, held their tips to two points on the door's surface. After a moment, the keys sank slowly into the door. Ti twisted them in turn, withdrew them. The door—a thick ponderous door—swung slowly into the room beyond. Ti motioned Telzey and Gaziel inside, followed them through.

"We're now within the computer," he said, "and this room, like the entire section, is heavily shielded. Not that we expect trouble. Only Linden and I have access here. No one else even knows where the Dramateer Room is. As my assistants-to-be, however, you should be introduced to it."

The room wasn't large. It was long, narrow, low-ceilinged. At the end nearest the door was a sunken control complex with two seats. Ti tapped the wall. "The computer extends downward for three levels from here. I don't imagine you've been behind a Martri stage before?"

They shook their heads.

"A good deal of mystery is made of it," Ti said. "But the difficulty lies in the basic programming of the computer. That takes a master! If anything at all is botched, the machine never quite recovers. Few Martri computers in existence might be said to approach perfection. This one comes perhaps closest to it, though it must operate on a much wider scale than any other built so far."

"You programmed it?" Telzey asked.

Ti looked surprised. "Of course! Who else could have been entrusted with it? It demanded the utmost of my skills and discernment. But as for the handling of the computer—the work of the dramateer—that isn't really complicated at all. Linden lacks genius but is technically almost as accomplished at it as I am. You two probably will be able to operate the computer efficiently and to direct Martridramas within a few months. After you've been here a year, I expect to find you composing your own dramas."

He stepped down into the control complex, settled into one of the seats, took a brimless cap of wire mesh from a recess and fitted it over his head. "A dramateer cap," he said. "It's not used here, but few dramas are directed from here. Our Martri Stage covers the entire island and the body of water immediately surrounding it, and usually Linden and I prefer to be members of the audience. You're aware that the computer has the capability of modifying a drama while it's being enacted. On occasion, such a modification could endanger the audience. When it happens, the caps enable us to override the computer. That's almost their only purpose."

"How does it work?" Gaziel asked.

Ti tapped the top of his head. "Through microcontacts in my skull," he said. "The dramateer usually verbalizes my instructions, but it's not necessary. The thought, if precise enough, is sufficient. It's interesting that no one knows what makes that possible."

He indicated the wall at the far end of the room with a nod. "A check screen. I'll show you a few of the forest puppets."

His hands flicked with practiced quickness about the controls, and a view appeared in the screen—a squat low building with sloping walls, standing in a wide clearing among trees. That must be the control fort Remiol and Eshan had talked about.

The screen flickered. Telzey felt a pang in the center of her forehead. It faded, returned. She frowned. She almost never got headaches. . . .

Image in the screen—heavily built creature digging in the ground with clawed feet. Gaziel watched Ti, lips slightly parted, blue eyes intent. Ti talking: "—no precise natural counterpart but we've given it a viable metabolism and, if you will, viable instincts. It's programmed to nourish itself, and does. Weight over two tons—"

The pain—a rather mild pain—in Telzey's head shifted to her temples. It might be an indication of something other than present tensions.

An inexperienced or clumsy attempt by a telepath to probe a resistant human mind could produce reactions which in turn produced the symptom of a moderately aching head.

And Linden was a clumsy psi.

It could be the human original he was trying to probe, Telzey thought, but it could as well be the Martri copy, whose head presumably would ache identically. Linden might be playing his own game—attempting to establish secret control over Ti's new tools before he had normal psi defenses to contend with. . . . Whichever she was, that could be a mistake! If she was resisting the attempt, then some buried psi part of her of which she hadn't been conscious was active—and was now being stimulated by use.

Let him keep on probing! It couldn't harm at all. . . .

"What do you think of that beauty?" Ti asked her with a benign smile.

A new thing in the screen. A thing that moved like a thick sheet of slowly flowing yellowish oil along the ground between

the trees. Two dark eyes bulged from the forward end. Telzey
cleared her throat. "Sort of repulsive," she remarked.

"Yes, and far from harmless. Hunger is programmed into
it, and it's no vegetarian. If we allowed it to satisfy its urges
indiscriminately, there'd be a constant need to replenish the
forest fauna. I'll impel it now into an attack on the fort."

The flowing mass abruptly shifted direction and picked up
speed. Ti tracked it through the forest for a minute or two,
then flicked the screen back to a view of the fort. Moments
later, the glider came out into the clearing, front end raised, a
fanged, oddly glassy-looking mouth gaping wide at its tip. It
slapped itself against the side of the fort. Gaziel said, "Could
it get in?"

Ti chuckled comfortably. "Yes, indeed! It can compress itself almost to paper thinness, and if permitted, it would soon
locate the gun slits and enter through one of them. But the
fort's well armed. When one of our self-sustaining monsters
threatens to slip from computer control, the fort is manned
and the rogue is directed or lured into attacking it. The guns
will destroy any of them, though it takes a good deal longer to
do than if they were natural animals of comparable size." He
smiled. "For them, too, I have plans, though those plans are
still far from fruition."

He shut off the screen, turned down a number of switches,
and got out of the control chair. "We're putting on a full
Martridrama after dinner tonight, in honor of your appearance among us," he told them. "Perhaps you'd like to select
one you think you'd enjoy seeing. If you'll come down here,
I'll show you how to scan through samples of our repertoire."

They stepped down into the pit, took the console seats. Ti
explained the controls, moved back, and stood watching their
faces as they began the scan. Telzey and Gaziel kept their
eyes fixed on the small screens before them, studied each
drama sample produced briefly, went on to the next. Several
minutes passed in silence, broken only by an intermittent
muted whisper of puppet voices from the screens. Finally Ti
asked blandly, "Have you found something you'd like?"

Telzey shrugged. "It all *seems* as if it might be interesting
enough," she said. "But it's difficult to tell much from these
samples." She glanced at Gaziel. "What do you think?"

Gaziel, smooth face expressionless, said, "Why don't you

pick one out, Ti? You'd make a better selection than we could."

Ti showed even white teeth in an irritated smile.

"You aren't easy to unsettle!" he said. "Very well, I'll choose one. One of my favorites to which I've added a few twists since showing it last." He looked at his watch. "You've seen enough for today. Run along and entertain yourself! Dinner will be in three hours. It will be a formal one, and we'll have company, so I want to see you come beautifully gowned and styled. Do you know your way back to your room from here?"

They said they did, followed him out of the Dramateer Room, watched as he sealed and locked the door. Then they started back to their room. As they turned into a passage on the next level up, they checked, startled.

5

The blue-haired woman Ti had called Challis stood motionless thirty feet away, looking at them. Pale eyes, pale face . . . the skin of Telzey's back began to crawl. Perhaps it was only the unexpectedness of the encounter, but she remembered how Ti had lost color when Challis first appeared; and the thought came that she might feel this way if she suddenly saw a ghost and knew what it was.

Challis lifted a hand now, beckoned to them. They started hesitantly forward. She turned aside as they came up, went to an open door, and through it. They glanced at each other.

"I think we'd better see what she wants," Telzey said quietly.

Gaziel nodded, looking quite as reluctant about it as Telzey felt. "Probably."

They went to the door. A narrow dim-lit corridor led off it. Challis was walking up the corridor, some distance away. They exchanged glances again.

"Let's go."

They slipped into the corridor, started after Challis. The

door closed silently behind them. They came out, after several corridor turns, into a low wide room, quite bare—the interior of a box. Diffused light poured from floor, ceiling, the four walls. The surfaces looked like highly polished metal but cast no reflections.

"Nothing reaches here," Challis said to them. "We can talk." She had a low musical voice which at first didn't seem to match her appearance, then did. "Don't be alarmed by me. I came here only to talk to you."

They looked at her a moment. "Where did you come from?" Gaziel asked.

"From inside."

"Inside?"

"Inside the machine. I'm usually there, or seem to be. I don't really give much attention to it. Now and then—not often, I believe—I'm told to come out."

"Who tells you to come out?" Telzey said carefully.

Challis' light-gray eyes regarded her.

"The minds," she said. "The machine thinks on many levels. Thinking forms minds. We didn't plan that. It developed. They're there; they do their work. That's the way they feel it should be. You understand?"

They nodded hesitantly.

"He knows they're there," Challis said. "He sees the indications. He can affect some of them. Many more are inaccessible to him at present, but it's been noted that he's again modified and extended the duplicative processes. He's done things that are quite new, and now he's brought in the new model who is one of you. The model's been analyzed and it was found that it incorporates a quality through which he should be able to gain access to any of the minds in the machine. That's not wanted. If the duplicate made of the model—the other of you—has the same quality, that's wanted even less. If it's been duplicated once, it can be duplicated many times. And he will duplicate it many times. It's not his way to make limited use of a successful model. He'll make duplicates enough to control every mind in the machine."

"*We* don't want that," Gaziel said.

Challis' eyes shifted to her.

"It won't happen," she said, "if he's unable to use either of you for his purpose. It's known that you have high resistive levels to programming, but it's questionable whether you can maintain those levels indefinitely. Therefore the model and its duplicate should remove themselves permanently from the area of the machine. That's the logical and most satisfactory solution."

Telzey glanced at Gaziel. "We'd very much like to do it," she said. "Can you help us get off the island?"

Challis frowned.

"I suppose there's a way to get off the island," she said slowly. "I remember other places."

"Do you remember where they keep the aircars here?" said Gaziel.

"Aircars?" Challis repeated. She looked thoughtful. "Yes, he has aircars. They're somewhere in the structure. However, if the model and the duplicate aren't able to leave the area, they should destroy themselves. The minds will provide you with opportunities for self-destruction. If you fail, direct procedures will be developed to delete you."

Telzey said after a moment, "But they won't help us get off the island?"

Challis shook her head. "The island is the Martri stage. Things come to it; things leave it. I remember other places. Therefore, there should be a way off it. The way isn't known. The minds can't help you in that."

"The aircars—"

"There are aircars somewhere in the structure. Their exact location isn't known."

Telzey said, "There's still another solution."

"What?"

"The minds could delete him instead."

"No, that's not a solution," said Challis. "He's essential in the maintenance of the universe of the machine. He can't be deleted."

"Who are you?" Gaziel asked.

Challis looked at her.

"I seem to be Challis. But when I think about it, as I'm doing at this moment, it seems it can't be. Challis knew many things I don't know. She helped him in the design of the machine. Her puppet designs were better than his own, though he's learned much more than she ever knew. And she was one of our most successful models herself. Many puppet lines were her copies, modified in various ways."

She paused reflectively.

"Something must have happened to Challis," she told them. "She isn't there now, except as I seem to be her. I'm a pattern of some of her copies in the machine, and no longer accessible to him. He's tried to delete me, but minds always deflect the deletion instructions while indicating they've been carried out. Now and then, as happened here, they make another copy of her in the vats, and I'm programmed to it and told what to do. That's disturbing to him."

Challis was silent for a moment again. Then she added, "It appears I've given you the message. Go back the way you came. Avoid doing what he intends you to do. If you can deactivate the override system, do it. When you have the opportunity, leave the area or destroy yourselves. Either solution will be satisfactory."

She turned away and started off across the glowing floor.

"Challis," said Gaziel.

Challis looked back.

"Do the minds know which of us two is the model?" Gaziel asked.

"That's of no concern to them now," said Challis.

She went on. They looked after her, at each other, turned back toward the corridor. Telzey's head still ached mildly. It continued to ache off and on for another hour. Then that stopped. She didn't mention it to Gaziel.

There were thirty-six people at dinner, most of them island employees. Telzey and Gaziel were introduced. No mention was made of a puppet double, and no one commented on their identical appearance, though there might have been a good deal of silent speculation. Telzey gathered from her table companions that they regarded themselves as highly privileged to be here and to be working for Dr. Ti. They were ardent Martriphiles and spoke of Ti's genius in reverent terms. Once she noticed Linden watching her from the other end of the table. She gave him a pleasant smile, and he looked away, expression unchanged.

Shortly after dinner, the group left the building by the main entrance. Something waited for them outside—a shell-like device, a miniature auditorium with curved rows of comfortable chairs. They found their places, Telzey sitting beside Gaziel, and the shell lifted into the air and went floating away across the estate. Night had come by then. The familiar magic of the starblaze hung above the island. White globe lights shone here and there among the trees. The shell drifted down presently to a point where the estate touched a narrow bay of the sea, and became stationary twenty feet above the ground. Ti and Linden, seated at opposite ends of the shell, took out override caps and fitted the woven mesh over their heads.

There was a single deep bell note. The anticipatory murmur talk ended abruptly. The starblaze dimmed out, and stillness closed about them. All light faded.

Then—a curtain shifting again—they looked out at the shore of a tossing sea, a great sun lifting above the horizon, and the white sails of a tall ship sweeping in toward them out of history. There was a sound in the air that was roar of sea and wail of wind and splendid music.

Ti's Martridrama had begun.

"I liked the first act," Telzey said judiciously.

"But the rest I'd sooner not have seen," said Gaziel.

Ti looked at them. The others of his emotionally depleted audience had gone off to wherever their quarters in the complex were. "Well, it takes time to develop a Martriphile," he observed mildly.

They nodded.

"I guess that's it," Telzey said.

They went to their room, got into their beds. Telzey lay awake a while, looking out through the big open window at tree branches stirring under the starblaze. There was a clean salt sea smell and night coolness on the breeze. She heard dim sounds in the distance. She shivered for a moment under the covers.

The Martridrama had been horrible. Ti played horrible games.

A throbbing set in at her temples. Linden was working late. This time, it lasted only about twenty minutes.

She slept.

She came awake again. Gaziel was sitting up in bed on the other side of the room. They looked at each other silently and without moving in the shadowed dimness.

A faint music had begun somewhere. It might be coming out of the walls of the room, or from beyond the window. They couldn't tell. But it was music they'd heard earlier that night, in the final part of the Martridrama. It swelled gradually, and the view outside the window began to blur, dimmed out by slow pulsing waves of cold drama light which spilled into the room and washed over the floor. A cluster of vague images flickered over the walls, then another.

They edged out of bed, met in the center of the room. For an instant, the floor trembled beneath them.

Telzey whispered unsteadily, "I guess Ti's putting us on stage!"

Gaziel gave her a look which said, *We'll hope it's just Ti!* "Let's see if we can get out of this."

They backed off toward the door. Telzey caught the knob, twisted, tugged. The knob seemed suddenly to melt in her hand, was gone.

"Over there!" Gaziel whispered.

There was blackness beyond the window now. A blackness which shifted and stirred. The outlines of the room were moving, began to flow giddily about them. Then it was no longer the room.

They stood on the path of a twisting ravine, lit fitfully by reddish flames lifting out of the rocks here and there, leaping over the ground and vanishing again. The upper part of the ravine was lost in shadows which seemed to press down closely on it. On either side of the path, drawn back from it only a little, was unquiet motion, a suggestion of shapes, outlines, which appeared to be never quite the same or in the same place from moment to moment.

They looked back. Something squat and black was walking up the path toward them, its outlines wavering here and there as if it were composed of dense smoke. They turned away from it, started along the path. It was wide enough to let them walk side by side, but not much wider.

Gaziel breathed, "I wish Ti hadn't picked this one!"

Telzey was wishing it, too. Perhaps they were in no real danger. Ti certainly shouldn't be willing to waste them if they made a mistake. But they'd seen Martridrama puppets die puppet deaths in this ravine tonight; and if the minds of which Challis had spoken existed and were watching, and if Ti was *not* watching closely enough, opportunities for their destruction could be provided too readily here.

"We'd better act exactly as if it's real!" Telzey murmured.

"I know."

To get safely out of the ravine, it was required to keep walking and not leave the path. The black death which followed wouldn't overtake them unless they stopped. Whatever moved along the sides of the ravine couldn't reach them on the path. There were sounds and near-sounds about them, whispers and a hungry whining, wisps of not quite audible laughter, and once a sharp snarl that seemed inches from Telzey's ear. They kept their eyes on the path, which mightn't be too stable, ignoring what could be noticed along the periphery of their vision.

It shouldn't go on much longer, Telzey told herself presently—and then a cowled faceless figure, the shape of a man but twice the height of a man, rose out of the path ahead and blocked their way.

They came to a startled stop. That figure hadn't appeared in the ravine scene they'd watched. They glanced back. The smoky black thing was less than twenty feet away, striding steadily closer. On either side, there was an abrupt eager clustering of flickering images. The cowled figure remained motionless. They went on toward it. As they seemed about to touch it, it vanished. But the other shapes continued to seethe about now in a growing fury of activity.

The ravine vanished.

They halted again—in a quiet, dim-lit passage, a familiar one. There was an open door twelve feet away. They went through it, drew it shut, were back in the room assigned to them. It looked ordinary enough. Outside the window, tree branches rustled in a sea wind under the starblaze. There were no unusual sounds in the air.

Telzey drew a long breath, murmured, "Looks like the show is over!"

Gaziel nodded. "Ti must have used his override to cut it short."

Their eyes met uneasily for a moment. There wasn't much question that somebody hadn't intended to let them get out of that scene alive! It hadn't been Ti; and it didn't seem very likely that it could have been Linden. . . .

Telzey sighed. "Well," she said, "everyone's probably had enough entertainment for tonight! We'd better get some sleep while we can."

6

Ti had a brooding look about him at the breakfast table. He studied their faces for some moments after they sat down, then inquired how they felt.

"Fine," said Telzey. She smiled at him. "Are just the three of us having breakfast here this morning?"

"Linden's at work," said Ti.

"We thought your wife might be eating with us," Gaziel told him.

Ti made a sound between a grunt and a laugh.

"She died during the night," he said. "I expected it. She never lasts long."

"Eh?" said Telzey.

"She was a defective puppet," Ti explained. "An early model, made in the image of my wife Challis, who suffered a fatal accident some years ago. A computer error which I've been unable to eradicate causes a copy of the puppet to be produced in the growth vats from time to time. It regards itself as Challis, and because of its physical similarity to her, I don't like to disillusion it or dispose of it." He shrugged. "I have a profound aversion to the thing, but its defects always destroy it again within a limited number of hours."

He gnawed his lip, observed dourly, "Your appetites seem undiminished! You slept well?"

They nodded. "Except for the Martri stuff, of course," said Gaziel.

"What was the purpose of that?" Telzey asked.

"A reaction test," said Ti. "It didn't disturb you?"

"It was scary enough," Telzey said, "We knew *you* didn't intend to kill us, but at the end it looked like the computer might be getting carried away. Did you have to override it?"

Ti nodded. "Twice, as a matter of fact! It's quite puzzling! That's a well-established sequence—it's been a long time since the computer or a puppet attempted a logic modification."

"Perhaps it was because we weren't programmed puppets,"

Gaziel suggested. "Or because one of us wasn't a puppet at all."

Ti shook his head. "Under the circumstances, that should make no difference." His gaze shifted from one to the other. For an instant, something unpleasant flickered in his eyes. "You may be almost too stable!" he remarked. "Well, we shall see—"

"What will we be doing today?" Telzey asked.

"I'm not certain," Ti said. "There may be various developments. You'll be on your own part of the time, at any rate, but don't go roaming around the estate. Stay in the building area where I can have you paged if I want you."

They nodded. Gaziel said, "There must be plenty of interesting things to see in the complex. We'll look around."

They had some quite definite plans for looking around. The longer Ti stayed busy with other matters during the following hours, the better. . . .

It didn't work out exactly as they'd hoped then. They'd finished breakfast and excused themselves. Gaziel had got out of her chair; Telzey was beginning to get out of hers.

There was something like a dazzling white flash inside her head.

And she was in darkness. Reclining in some kind of very comfortable chair—comfortable except for the fact that she was securely fastened to it. Cool stillness about her. Then a voice.

It wasn't mind-talk, and it wasn't sound picked up by her ears. Some stimulation was being applied to audio centers of her brain.

"You must relax and not resist," she heard. "You've been brought awake because you must try consciously not to resist."

Cold fear welled through her. Ti had showed them the programming annex of the Martri computer yesterday. She was there now—they were trying to program her! Something was fastened about her skull. Feelings like worm-crawlings stirred in her head.

She tried to push the feelings away. They stopped.

"You must relax," said the voice in her audio centers. "You must not resist. Think of relaxing and of not resisting."

The worm-crawlings began again. She pushed at them.

"You are not thinking of relaxing and not resisting," said the voice. "Try to think of that."

So the programming annex knew what she was and was not thinking. She was linked into the computer. Ti had said that if a thought was specific enough—

"We've been trying for almost two hours to get you programmed," Ti said. "What was your experience?"

"Well, I couldn't have been awake for more than the last ten minutes," Telzey said, her expression sullen. "I don't know what happened the rest of the time."

Linden said from a console across the room, "We want to know what happened while you were awake."

"It felt like something was pushing around inside my head," Telzey said.

"Nothing else?" said Ti.

"Oh, there was a kind of noise now and then."

"Only a noise? Can you describe it?"

She shrugged. "I don't know how to describe it. It was just a noise. That was inside my head, too." She shivered. "I didn't like any of it! I don't want to be programmed, Ti!"

"Oh, you'll have to be programmed," Ti said reasonably. "Let's be sensible about this. Were you trying to resist the process?"

"I didn't know how to resist it," Telzey said. "But I certainly didn't want it to happen!"

Ti rubbed his chin, looking at her, asked Linden, "How does the annex respond now?"

"Perfectly," Linden said.

"We'll see how the other subject reacts. Telzey, you wait outside—that door over there. Linden will conduct you out of the annex in a few minutes."

Telzey found Gaziel standing in the adjoining room. Their eyes met. "Did you get programmed?" Gaziel asked.

Telzey shook her head.

"No. Some difficulty with the annex—almost like it didn't want me to be programmed."

Gaziel's eyelids flickered; she nodded quickly, came over, watching the door, slipped something into Telzey's dress pocket, stepped back. "I suppose it's my turn now," she said.

"Yes," Telzey said. "They were talking about it. It's like little worms pushing around inside your head, and there's a noise. Not too bad really, but you won't like it. You'll wish there were a way you could override it."

Gaziel nodded again.

"I hope it won't take with me either," she said. "The idea of walking around programmed is something I can't stand!"

"If it doesn't work on you, maybe Ti will give up," Telzey said.

The door opened and Linden came out. He looked at Gaziel, jerked his thumb at the doorway. "Dr. Ti wants to see you now," he told her.

"Good luck!" Telzey said to Gaziel. Gaziel nodded, walked into the other room. Linden closed the door on her.

"Come along," he said to Telzey. "Dr. Ti's letting you have the run of the building, but he doesn't want you in the programming annex while he's working on the other one."

They started from the room. Telzey said, "Linden—"

"Dr. Linden," Linden said coldly.

Telzey nodded. "Dr. Linden. I know you don't like me—"

"Quite right," Linden said. "I don't like you. You've brought me nothing but trouble with Dr. Ti since you first showed up in Draise! In particular, I didn't appreciate that psi trick you pulled on me."

"Well, that was self-defense," Telzey said reasonably. "What would you do if you found someone trying to pry around in your mind? That is, if you could do what I did. . . ." She looked reflective. "I don't suppose you can, though."

Linden gave her an angry look.

"But even if you don't like me, or us," Telzey went on, "you really should prefer it if Ti can't get us programmed. You're important to him because you're the only telepath he has. But if it turns out we're both psis, or even only the original one, and he can control us, you won't be nearly so important anymore."

Linden's expression was watchful now. "You're suggesting that I interfere with the process?" he said sardonically.

Telzey shrugged. "Well, whatever you think you can do."

Linden made a snorting sound.

"I'll inform Dr. Ti of this conversation," he told her. He opened another door. "Now get out of my sight!"

She got. Linden had been pushed as far as seemed judicious at present.

She took the first elevator she saw to the third floor above ground level, went quickly to their room. The item Gaziel had placed in her pocket was a plastic package the size of her thumb. She unsealed it, unfolded the piece of paper inside, which was covered with her private shorthand. She read:

> Comm office on level seven, sect. eighteen. It's there. Usable? Janitor-guard, Togelt, buttered up, won't bother you. Comm man, Rodeen, blurs up like Remiol on stim. Can be hypnoed straight then! No one else around. Got paged before finished. Carry on. Luck.
>
> Me

Telzey pulled open the wardrobe, got out a blouse and skirt combination close enough to what Gaziel had been wearing to pass inspection by Togelt and Rodeen, went to a mirror and began arranging her hair to match that of her double. Gaziel had made good use of the morning! Locating a communicator with which they might be able to get out a message had been high on their immediate priority list, second only to discovering where the island's air vehicles were kept.

Telzey went still suddenly, eyes meeting those of her mirror image. Then she nodded gently to herself. The prod she'd given Linden had produced quick results! He *was* worried about the possibility that Ti might acquire one or two controlled psis who could outmatch him unless he established his own controls first.

Her head was aching again.

Preparations completed; she got out a small map of the central complex she'd picked up in an office while Ti was conducting them around the day before. It was informative quite as much in what it didn't show as in what it did. Sizable sections of the upper levels obviously weren't being shown. Neither was most of the area occupied by the Martri computer, including the Dramateer Room. Presumably these were all places barred to Ti's general personnel. That narrowed down the search for aircars considerably. They should be in one of the nonindicated places which was also near the outer wall of the complex.

Rodeen was thin, sandy-haired, in his early twenties. He smiled happily at sight of Telzey. His was a lonely job; and Gaziel had left him with the impression that he'd been explaining the island's communication system to her when Ti had her paged. Telzey let him retain the impression. A few minutes later, she inquired when he'd last been off Ti's island. Rodeen's eyes glazed over. He was already well under the influence.

She hadn't worked much with ordinary hypnosis because there'd been no reason for it. Psi, when it could be used, was more effective, more dependable. But in her general study of the mind, she'd learned a good deal about the subject. Rodeen, of course, was programmed against thinking about the communicator which would reach other points on Orado; it took about twenty minutes to work through that. By then, he was no longer in the least aware of where he was or what he was doing. He opened a safe, brought out the communicator, set it on a table.

Telzey looked it over, asked Rodeen a few questions. Paused then. Quick footsteps came along the passage outside the office. She went to the door.

"What did Togelt think when he saw you?" she asked.

"That I was your twin, of course," Gaziel said. "Amazing similarity!"

"Ti sure gave up on you fast!"

Gaziel smiled briefly. "You sure got that programming annex paralyzed! Nothing would happen at all—that's why he gave up. How did you override it?"

"It knew what I was thinking. So I thought the situation was an override emergency which should be referred to the computer director," Telzey said. "There was a kind of whistling in my head then, which probably was the director. I referred to the message we got from Challis and indicated that letting us be programmed by Ti couldn't be to the advantage of the Martri minds. Apparently, they saw it. The annex went out of business almost at once. Did Ti call for Linden again?" Her headache had stopped some five minutes ago.

Gaziel nodded. "We'll have some time to ourselves again— Ti'll page us when he wants us."

She'd come in through the door. Her gaze went to the table, and she glanced quickly at Telzey's face. "So you found it. We can't use it?"

"Not until we get the key that turns it on," Telzey said, "and probably only Ti knows where it is. Nobody else ever uses the gadget, not even Linden."

"No good to us at the moment then." Gaziel looked at Rodeen, who was smiling thoughtfully at nothing. "In case we get hold of the key," she said, "let's put in a little posthypnotic work on him so we can just snap him back into the trances another time. . . ."

They left the office shortly, having restored Rodeen to a normal condition, with memories now only of a brief but enjoyable conversation he'd had with the twins.

Telzey glanced at her watch. "Past lunch time," she remarked. "But Ti may stay busy a while today. Let's line up the best spots to look for aircars."

The complex map was consulted. They set off for another upper-level section.

"That blur-and-hypnotize them approach," said Gaziel, "might be a way to get ourselves a gun—if they had armed guards standing around."

Telzey glanced at her. So far, they'd seen no armed guards in the complex. With Ti's employees as solidly programmed as they were, he didn't have much need even for locked doors. "The troops he keeps to hunt down rambunctious forest things have guns, of course," she said. "But they're pretty heavy caliber."

Gaziel nodded. "I was thinking of something more inconspicious—something we could shove under Ti's or Linden's nose if it got to be that kind of situation."

"We'll keep our eyes open," Telzey said. "But we should be able to work out a better way than that."

"Several, I think," said Gaziel. She checked suddenly. "Speaking of keeping our eyes open—"

"Yes?"

"That's an elevator door over there, isn't it?"

"That's what their elevator doors look like," Telzey agreed. She paused. "You think that one doesn't show on the map?"

"Not as I remember it," Gaziel said. "Let's check—section three seventeen dash three."

They spread the map out on the floor, knelt beside it. Telzey shifted the scale enlargement indicator to the section number. The map surface went blank; then a map of the section appeared. "We're—here!" said Gaziel, finger tapping the map. "And, right, that elevator doesn't show—doesn't exist for programmed personnel. Let's see where it goes!"

They opened the door, looked inside. There was an on-off

switch, nothing to indicate where the elevator would take them. "Might step out into Ti's office," Telzey said.

Gaziel shrugged. "He knows we're exploring around."

"Yes. But he could be in a pretty sour mood right now." Telzey shrugged in turn. "Well, come on!"

They stepped into the elevator. The door closed, and Telzey turned the switch. Some seconds passed. The door opened again.

They stood motionless, looking out and around. Gaziel glanced over at Telzey, shook her head briefly.

"It can't be as easy as *that!*" she murmured.

Telzey bit her lip. "Unless it's locked . . . or unless there's a barrier field that won't pass it. . . ."

The door had opened at the back of a large sun-filled porch garden. Seemingly, at least, the porch was open to the cloudless sky beyond. There were rock arrangements, small trees, flower beds stirring in a warm breeze. Near the far end was a graveled open area—and a small aircar was parked on it. No one was in sight.

No, Telzey thought, escape from Ti's island couldn't be so simple a matter! There must be some reason why they couldn't use the aircar. But they had to find out what the reason was. . . .

They moved forward warily together, a few steps, emerged from the elevator, looked around, listening, tensed. Gaziel started forward again. Telzey suddenly caught her arm, hauled hard. Back they went stumbling into the elevator.

"What's the matter?" Gaziel whispered.

Telzey passed her hand over her mouth, shook her head. "Close!" she muttered. "The sun—"

Gaziel looked. Her eyes widened in comprehension. "Should be overhead, this time of day!"

"Yes, it should . . ." It wasn't. Its position indicated it might be midmorning or midafternoon on the garden porch.

The garden porch—a Martri stage.

"They set it up for us!" Gaziel murmured. "We asked Challis where we could find aircars."

Telzey nodded. "So they spotted us coming and spun in a scene from some drama—to get us out there, on stage!"

"They almost did. . . . Look at it now!" Gaziel said softly. "Nothing's moving."

The garden porch had gone still, dead still. No eddy of air

disturbed the flower beds; no leaf lifted. There was total silence about them.

"They've stopped the scene," Telzey whispered. "Waiting to see if we won't still try to reach the car."

"And find out we've become part of the action! Wonder what— It's moving again!"

The garden growth stirred lazily, as before. A breeze touched their faces. Some seconds passed. Then they heard a hoarse shout, a high cry of fear, and, moments later, running steps. A young man and a young woman burst into view from behind a cluster of shrubs, darted toward the aircar.

The Martri scene began to fade. Off to the left, another man was rising out of concealment, holding a gun in both hands. He took unhurried aim at the pair as they pulled open the door of the car. Then flame tore through the two bodies, continued to slash into them as they dropped writhing to the ground, dimming out swiftly now with everything about them.

Telzey turned the elevator switch. The door slid shut. They looked at each other.

"If you hadn't noticed the sun!" Gaziel said. She drew in a long breath. "If we'd— The computer would hardly have had to modify that scene at all to get us deleted!"

"Wish those minds weren't in quite such a hurry about that," Telzey said.

The elevator door opened. They stepped out into the hall from which they'd entered it.

7

"Oh, certainly we have permanent Martri stages here in the complex," Ti said at lunch. "They're generally off limits to personnel, but you two are quite free to prowl about there if you like. The equipment's foolproof. Remind me to give you a chart tomorrow to help you locate some of them."

He appeared affable, though bemused. Now and then he regarded them speculatively. He'd spent all morning, he told them, trying to track down the problem in the programming annex. The annex, a relatively simple piece of Martri equipment, was Linden's responsibility; but Linden was limited.

Ti shrugged.

"I'll work it out," he said. "It's possible I'll have to modify the overall programming approach used on you. Meanwhile—well, Linden has business offices on the level above your room. I'd like you to go there after you finish. He's to carry your general indoctrination a step further this afternoon. Go up the stairs nearest your room and turn left. You won't have any trouble finding him."

They didn't. They came to a main office first, which was a sizable one where half a dozen chatty and cheerful-looking young women were at work. One of them stood up and came over.

"Dr. Linden?" she said. "Oh, yes. He's expecting you."

They followed her through another room to Linden's private office. He arose behind his desk as they came in.

"Dr. Ti informed me you were on your way here," he said. He looked at the young woman. "I'll be out of the office a while. Take care of things."

"How long do you expect to be gone, sir?" she asked.

"Between one and two hours." Linden gave Telzey and Gaziel a twisted smile. "Let's go!"

He led them up a narrow passage to an alcove where sunlight flooded in through colored windows. Here was a door. Linden unlocked it but didn't open it immediately.

"I'll explain the situation," he said, turning back to them. "I told Dr. Ti in Draise that Telzey might become dangerous, and advised him to have her destroyed. But he was intrigued by the possibilities he felt he saw in her, and in creating puppet doubles of her." Linden shrugged. "Well, that's his affair. He's been attempting to shake you up psychologically—Martri programming takes hold best on minds that have been reduced to a state of general uncertainty. However, his methods haven't worked very well. And he now suspects you may have deliberately caused the malfunction of the programming annex this morning. So he's decided to try a different approach—and for once in this matter, I find myself in complete accord with him!"

"What's the new approach?" Telzey asked guardedly.

Linden smiled.

"We have devices in the room behind that door," he said,

"which were designed to put difficult subjects into a docile and compliant frame of mind. I'm happy to say that various phases of the process are accompanied by intense physical pain—and believe me, you're getting the full treatment!"

Telzey said, "One of us is Gaziel. She hasn't done anything to you. Why do you want to give her the full treatment?"

Linden shrugged. "Why not? Subjectively you're both Telzey, and as far as I'm concerned, you're equally insufferable. You'll find out which of you is Telzey in fact when you're supposed to. I'll make no distinctions now. When I feel you've been sufficiently conditioned, I'll put you through the psi depressant procedure again to make sure no problems begin to develop in that area. Then I'll report to Dr. Ti that his subjects are ready for further programming sessions."

He smiled at Telzey.

"You," he said, "had the effrontery to suggest that it would be to my advantage if Dr. Ti gave up his plan to program the two of you. I don't agree. He feels now that the experiment probably will fail as such, but will produce valuable new information. So he'll continue with it until neither of you has enough mind left to be worth further study. I see nothing undesirable in that prospect!"

He opened the door he'd unlocked, glanced back down the passage in the direction of the offices.

"This kind of thing could disturb the illusions of the work staff," he remarked. "Subjects experiencing the docility treatment make a remarkable amount of noise. But the place is thoroughly soundproofed, so that's no problem. You're at liberty to yowl your heads off in there. I'll enjoy listening to it. In you go!"

He took each of them by an arm and shoved them through the door into the room beyond. He followed, drawing the door shut behind him, and locked it from inside. As he started to turn back toward them, Telzey dropped forward and wrapped herself around his ankles. Linden staggered off balance and came down, half on top of her. Gaziel came down on top of him.

It was a brisk scramble. Linden was somewhat awkward but big enough and strong enough to have handled either of them readily. Together, hissing, clawing for his eyes, clinging to his arms, kicking at his legs, they weren't being at all readily handled. They rolled across the room in a close-locked, rapidly shifting tangle, Linden trying to work an arm free and making inarticulate sounds of surprised fury. A table tipped over; a variety of instruments which had been standing on it crashed to the floor. Telzey saw one of them within reach, let go of Linden, snatched it up—mainly plastic but heavy—slammed it down on Linden's skull. He yelled. She swung down again with both hands, as hard as she could. The gadget broke, and Linden lay still.

"His keys—" she gasped.

"Got them!" Gaziel held up a flat purse.

They went quickly through Linden's pockets, found nothing else they could use. He was breathing noisily but hadn't moved again. "We'll just leave him locked in here," Telzey said as they scrambled to their feet. "That's a solid door—and he said the place was soundproof. . . ."

They unlocked the door, drew it cautiously open. Everything was quiet. They slipped out, locked the door, started down the passage. Somewhere another door opened; they heard feminine voices, turned back and ducked into the alcove across from the door.

"Once we're past the office area, we should be able to make it downstairs all right," Telzey said softly.

Gaziel studied her a moment, lips pursed. "Now we start them thinking we're hiding out in the forest, eh?"

"Yes. Looks like the best move, doesn't it?"

Gaziel nodded. "Wish we'd had a few more hours to prepare for it, though. Getting to the aircars is likely to be a problem."

"I know. It can't be helped."

"No," Gaziel agreed. "Between Linden and Ti planning to mess up our minds and the Martri computer waiting around to introduce some fancy deletion procedure, we'd better try to clear out of here the first chance we get! And this is it."

The side door to Linden's armored car opened to the third key Telzey tried. They slipped inside, drew the door shut.

Telzey settled into the driver's seat. "I'll get it started. Look around and see what he has here."

"Handguns he has here," Gaziel announced a moment later.

"A kind we can use?"

"Well, they're heavy things. I'll find out how they work."

There were clicking noises as she checked one of the guns. The car engine came to life. Telzey eased the vehicle back from the wall of the building, turned it around. It went off quickly across the lawn toward the nearest stand of garden trees. Gaziel looked over at her. "It handles all right?"

"It handles fine! Beautiful car. I'll come up on the taloaks from the other side."

"We can use the guns," Gaziel said. "I'll tie two of them to my belt for now. Nothing much else."

Taloaks made great climbing trees, and a sizable grove of them stretched to within a hundred yards of the residential area of the main building complex. Linden's car slipped up on the trees from the forest side of the estate, edged in among thickets of ornamental ground cover, stopped in the center of one of the densest clusters of growth. Its side door opened. Telzey climbed from the driver's seat to the top of the door, then onto the top of the car, followed by Gaziel. Each of them now had one of the big handguns Gaziel had discovered fastened to her dress belt. A thick taloak branch hung low over the car. They scrambled up to it, moved on.

Some five minutes later, they sat high in a tree near the edge of the grove, straddling branches six feet apart. They could watch much of the ground in front of the building through the leaves, were safely out of sight themselves. So far, there'd been no indication of activity in the area.

"It might be a while before they start looking for Linden," Gaziel said presently.

"Unless Ti checks in to see how our indoctrination is coming along," Telzey said.

"Yes, he's likely—"

Gaziel's voice broke off. Telzey looked over at her. She sat still, frozen, staring down at Linden's gun which she was holding in both hands.

"I'm sorry," Telzey said after a moment. "I wasn't really sure myself until just now."

Gaziel slowly refastened the gun to her belt, lifted her head.

"I'm nothing," she said, gray-faced. "A copy! A wirehead."

"You're me," Telzey said, watching her.

Gaziel shook her head. "I'm not you. You felt me get that order?"

Telzey nodded. "Ti's working through the computer. You

were to take control of me—use the gun if you had to—then
get me and Linden's car back to the main entrance."

"And I'd have done it!" Gaziel said. "I was about to point
the gun at you. You canceled the order—"

"Yes. I blanked out the computer contact."

Gaziel drew a ragged breath. "So you're back to being a
psi," she said. "How did that happen?"

"Linden's been trying to probe me. Off and on since yesterday. He pushed open a few channels finally. I finished doing
the rest of it about an hour ago."

Gaziel nodded. "And you took him over after you knocked
him out. What's the real situation now?"

Telzey said, "Ti did check. He had his own key to the treatment rooms. I woke Linden up and had him tell Ti a story
that got things boiling. What it amounts to is that we put guns
on Linden and got his personal standard communicator from
him before we knocked him out. We plan to find a spot in the
forest where we can hole up in his car and call for help. So
they're coming after us with their other armored cars—eleven
of them—in case the order Ti just gave you doesn't bring us
back."

Gaziel stared at her a moment, face still ashen. "Ti's going
with them?"

"Yes. And he's taking Linden along. They're about to start.
I'm still in contact with Linden, of course, and I know how
to get to the aircars. But they've stationed some guards at key
points in the complex. It will take us some time to maneuver
around those, and if we're seen, Ti could come back with his
patrols to stop us. So we have to make sure they can't get
back." She added, "There they are now!"

A groundcar swept around the curve of the building complex. Others followed at fifty-yard intervals. They arrowed
across the lawns in the direction of the forest wall, vanished
behind trees. Telzey said, "Ti and Linden are in five and six.
We can start down." She looked at Gaziel. "You are coming
with me, aren't you?"

"Oh, I'm coming with you!" Gaziel said. "I'll help any way
I can. I simply want all this to stop!"

8

Telzey locked the last control into position, pushed her hair back out of her face, looked over at Gaziel watching her from the edge of the console pit. A low heavy humming filled the Dramateer Room. "We're set," she said.

"Any detectable reaction from the minds yet?" asked Gaziel.

Telzey bit her lip reflectively. "Well, they're here, all right!" she said. "Around us. I can feel them. Like a whole army. Spooky! But they're just watching, I think. They haven't tried to interfere, so it doesn't seem they're going to be a problem. After all, we are getting out. It's what they wanted, and they seem to understand that we're doing it." She added, "Not that I'd like to tempt them by walking across one of their stages! But we won't have to do that."

"Just what have you been doing?" Gaziel said. "I couldn't begin to follow it."

"I couldn't either," Telzey said. "Linden did it. I sort of watched myself go through the motions." She flexed her fingers, looked at them. "Ti's forest things have cut the groundcars off from the gate and are chasing them up to the fort. One of the cars—well, they caught it. Ti and Linden already are in the fort. Ti's tried to contact the main complex, but the comm line leads through the computer and it's been cut off there. He knows the computer must be doing it, of course, and he's tried to override."

"The override system's deactivated?"

"That's the *first* thing we did," Telzey said. "They'll need a calculated minimum of thirty-two minutes to wipe out the forest puppets from the fort."

"That will get us to the aircars?"

"It should, easily. But we'll have a good deal more time. The first groundcar that comes back through the gate into the estate will start up a section of a Ti Martridrama—the third act of *Armageddon Five.* That's about what it sounds like, and its stage is the whole estate except for the central building complex. Ti won't be able to get here until Act Three's played out —and it takes over an hour. We want to keep him bottled up as long as possible, of course—"

She jerked suddenly, went still for a moment, shook her head.

"Linden just died!" she said then. "Ti shot him. He must have realized finally I had Linden under control. Well, it shouldn't change matters much now."

She got out of the console chair. "Come on! Mainly we'll have to be a little careful. I know where the guards are, but it'll be better if we don't run into anybody else either."

It took them eighteen minutes to work their way unseen through the building, and get into the aircar depot. A line of supply trucks stood there, four smaller aircars. They got into one of the cars. The roof of the depot opened as Telzey lifted the car toward it. The car halted at that point.

From a car window, they aimed Linden's guns at the power section of the nearest truck. After some seconds, it exploded, and the trucks next to it were instantly engulfed in flames. A chain reaction raced along the line of vehicles. They closed the window, went on up. Nobody was going to follow them from Ti's island. The energy field overhead dissolved at their approach, closed again below them. The car went racing off across the sunlit sea toward the Southern Mainland.

Gaziel sighed beside Telzey, laid the gun she'd been using down on the seat.

"I did have the thought," she said, "that if I shot you now and pushed you out, I could be Telzey Amberdon."

Telzey nodded.

"I knew you'd be having the thought," she said, "because I would have had it. And I knew you wouldn't do it then. Because I wouldn't do it."

"No," Gaziel said. "Only one of us can be the original. That's not your fault." She smiled, lazily, for the first time in an hour. "Am I dying, Telzey?"

"No," Telzey said. "You're going to sleep, other me. Don't fight it."

Some six weeks later, Telzey sat at a small table in a lounge of the Orado City Space Terminal, musing on information she'd received a few hours before.

It happened now and then that some prominent citizen of the Federation didn't so much disappear as find himself becoming gradually erased. It might be reported for a while that he was traveling, had been seen in one place or another, and eventually then that he'd settled down in quiet retirement, nobody seemed to know quite where. Meanwhile his enterprises were drifting into other hands, his properties dissolved, his name was mentioned with decreasing frequency. In the end, even former personal acquaintances seemed almost to forget he'd existed.

Thus it would be with Wakote Ti. He'd demanded a public trial. With his marvelous toys taken from him and an end made to the delights of unrestricted experimentation, he'd felt strongly that at least the world must be made aware of the full extent of his genius. The Federation's Psychology Service, which sometimes seemed the final arbiter on what was good for the Federation and sometimes not, decreed otherwise. The world would be told nothing, and Ti would be erased. He'd remain active, however; the Service always found a use for genius of any kind.

"What about all the new principles he discovered?" Telzey had asked Klayung, her Service acquaintance. "He must have been way ahead of anyone else there."

"To the best of our knowledge," said Klayung, "he was very far ahead of anyone else."

"Will that be suppressed now?"

"Not indefinitely. His theories and procedures are being carefully recorded. But they won't be brought into use for a while. Some toys seem best reserved for wiser children than we have around generally at present."

It was on record that Ti had deeded a private island to the planetary government, which would turn it into the site of a university. The illusory bank accounts of his innocent employees had acquired sudden reality. The less innocent employees were in Rehabilitation. His puppets and Martri equipment had disappeared.

And Gaziel—

Telzey watched a girl in a gray business suit come into the lounge, sent out a light thought to her.

"Over here!"

Acknowledgment returned as lightly. The girl came up to the table, sat down across from Telzey.

"You're taller than I am now, aren't you?" Telzey said.

Gaziel smiled. "By about half an inch."

Taller, more slender. The hollows under the cheekbones were more pronounced. There'd been a shift in the voice tones.

"They tell me I'll go on changing for about a year before I'm the way I want to be," Gaziel said. "There'll still be a good deal of similarity between us then, but no one would think I'm your twin." She regarded Telzey soberly. "I thought I didn't really want to see you again before I left. Now I'm glad I asked you to meet me here."

"So am I," Telzey said.

"I've become the sort of psi you are," said Gaziel. "Ti guessed right about that." She smiled briefly. "Some of it's surprised the Service a little."

"I knew it before we left the island," Telzey said. "You had everything I had. It just hadn't come awake."

"Why didn't you tell me?"

"I didn't dare do anything about you myself. I just got you to the Service as quickly as I could."

Gaziel nodded slowly. "I was on the edge then, wasn't I? I remember it. Have they told you how I've been doing?"

"No. They wouldn't. They said that if you wanted me to know, you'd tell me."

"I see." Gaziel was silent a moment. "Well, I want you to know. I hated you for a while. It wasn't reasonable, but I felt you were really the horrid changeling who'd pushed me out of *my* life, away from *my* family and friends. That was even after they'd taken the puppet contacts out of my head. I could think of explanations why Ti had planted them there, in the real Telzey." She smiled. "We're quite ingenious, aren't we?"

"Yes, we are," Telzey said.

"I got past that finally. I knew I wasn't Telzey and never had been. I was Gaziel, product of Wakote Ti's last and most advanced experiment. Then, for a while again, I was tempted. By that offer. I could become Gaziel Amberdon, Telzey's identical twin, newly arrived on Orado—step into a ready-made family, a ready-made life, a ready-made lie. Everything really could be quite simple for me. That was a cruel offer you made me, Telzey."

"Yes, it was cruel," Telzey said. "You had to have a chance to see if it was what you wanted."

"You knew I wouldn't want it?"

"I knew, all right. You'd have stayed a copy then, even if no one else guessed it."

Gaziel nodded. "I'm thanking you for the offer now. It did help me decide to become Gaziel who'll be herself and nobody's copy."

"I'd like to think," Telzey told her, "that this isn't the last time we'll be meeting."

"When I'm free of the Telzey pattern and have my own pattern all the way, I'll want to meet you again," Gaziel said. "I'll look you up." She regarded Telzey a moment, smiled. "In three or four years, I think."

"What will you be doing?"

"I'll work for the Service a while. Not indefinitely. After that, I'll see. Did you know I was one of Ti's heirs?"

"One of his heirs?"

"He isn't dead, of course. I drew my inheritance in advance. I used your legal schooling and found I could make out a rather strong case for paternal responsibility on Ti's part toward me. It was quite a lot of money, but he didn't argue much about it. I think I frighten him now. He's in a nervous condition anyway."

"What about?" Telzey said.

"Well, that Martri computer he had installed on the island is supposedly deactivated. The Service feels it's a bit too advanced for any general use at present. But Ti complains that Challis still comes around now and then. I wouldn't know—nobody else has run into her so far. It seems he arranged for the fatal accident the original Challis had. . . ." Gaziel glanced at her watch, stood up. "Time to go aboard. Goodbye, Telzey!"

"Good-bye," Telzey said. She looked after Gaziel as she turned away. Klayung, who wouldn't discuss Gaziel otherwise, had said thoughtfully, "By the time she's through with herself, she'll be a remarkably formidable human being—"

Gaziel checked suddenly, looked back. "Poor old Ti!" she said, laughing. "He didn't really have much of a chance, did he?"

"Not against the two of us," Telzey said. "Whatever he tried, we'd have got him one way or another."

Resident Witch

1

Telzey checked in at the Morrahall Hotel in Orado City that evening, had an early dinner, and thereupon locked herself into her room. The impression she'd left at Pehanron College was that she would be spending the night with her family. Her parents, on the other hand, naturally assumed she was at the college. She'd arranged with the ComWeb Service to have calls coming in at the college, at home, or to her car, transferred to the hotel room—if the caller, having been informed that she was busy and much preferred not to be disturbed before morning, felt there was justification enough for intruding on her privacy.

The semifinals of the annual robochess district championship series had begun, and she was still well up among the players. There should be two or three crucial games tonight, very little sleep. She wanted *all* the seclusion she could get.

She got into a casual outfit, settled down at the set, dialed herself into the series. Five minutes later, she was fed an opening move, an easy-looking one. She countered breezily. Six moves on, she was perspiring and trying to squirm out of an infernally ingenious trap. Out of it, though not unscathed, just ahead of deadline, she half closed a rather nasty little trap of her own.

Time passed in blissful absorption.

Then the ComWeb rang.

Telzey started, frowned, glanced at the instrument. It rang again. She pushed the Time Out button on the set, looked at her watch, switched on the ComWeb. "Yes?" she said.

"A caller requests override, Miss Amberdon," the Com-Web told her.

"Who is it?"

"The name is Wellan Dasinger."

"All right." Telzey clicked in nonvisual send, and Dasinger's lean tanned face appeared in the screen. "I'm here," she said. "Hello, Dasinger."

"Hello, Telzey. Are we private?"

"As private as we can be," she assured him. Dasinger was the head of Kyth Interstellar, a detective agency to which she'd given some assistance during the past year, and which in turn was on occasion very useful to her.

"I need information," he said. "Quite urgently—in your special study area. I'd like to come out to Pehanron and talk to you. Immediately, if possible." This was no reference to her law studies. Dasinger knew she was a psi; but neither he nor she referred to psi matters directly on a ComWeb. He added, "I realize it can't be the most convenient hour for you."

Dasinger wasn't given to overstatement. If he said a matter was quite urgent, it was as urgent as matters could get. Telzey depressed the Concede button on the robochess set, thereby taking herself out of the year's series. The set clicked off. "The hour's convenient, Dasinger," she said. "So is the location."

"Eh?"

"I'm not at the college. I took a room at the Morrahall for the night. You're at the agency?"

"I am." The Kyth offices were four city block complexes away. "Can I send someone over for you?"

"I'll be down at the desk in five minutes," Telzey told him.

She slipped into sportswear, fitted on a beret, slung her bag from her shoulder, and left the room.

There were three of them presently in Dasinger's private conference room. The third one was a Kyth operator Telzey hadn't met before, a big blond man named Corvin Wergard.

"What we want," Dasinger was saying, "is a telepath, a mind-reader—the real thing. Someone absolutely dependable. Someone who will do a fast, precise job for a high fee, and won't be too fussy about the exact legality of what he's involved in or a reasonable amount of physical risk. Can you

put us in contact with somebody like that? Some acquaintance?"

Telzey said hesitantly, "I don't know. It wouldn't be an acquaintance; but I *may* be able to find somebody like that for
you."

"We've tried the listed professionals," Wergard told her.
"Along with some unlisted ones who were recommended to
us. Mind-readers; people with telepathic devices. None of
them would be any good here."

Telzey nodded. No one like that was likely to be much
good anywhere. The good ones stayed out of sight. She said,
"It might depend on exactly what you want the telepath to do,
why you want him to do it. I know it won't be anything un-
ethical, but he'll want to be told more than that."

Dasinger said, "It may concern a murder already carried
out, or a murder that's still to come. If it's the last, we want to
prevent it. Unfortunately, there's very little time. Would you
like to see the file on the case? It's a short one."

Telzey would. It was brought to her.

The file was headed: *Selk Marine Equipment.* Which was a
company registered on Cobril, the water world eighteen hours
from Orado. The brothers Noal and Larien Selk owned the
company, Larien having been involved in it for only the past
six years. For the past four years, however, he alone had been
active in the management. Noal, who'd founded the company,
had been traveling about the Hub during that time, maintaining a casual connection with the business.

A week ago, Noal had contacted the Kyth Agency's branch
on Cobril. He'd returned unexpectedly, found indications that
Larien was syphoning off company funds, and apparently in-
vesting them in underworld enterprises on Orado. He wanted
the agency to start tracing the money on Orado, stated he
would arrive there in a few days with the evidence he'd accu-
mulated.

He hadn't arrived. Two days ago, Hishee Selk, Larien's
wife, appeared at the agency's Cobril branch. She said Larien
had implied to her that Noal had tried to make trouble for
him and would pay for it. From his hints, she believed Larien
had arranged to have Noal kidnapped and intended to murder
him. She wanted the agency to find Noal in time to save his
life.

The Selk file ended there. Visual and voice recordings of

the three principals were included. Telzey studied the images, listened to the voices. There wasn't much obvious physical resemblance between the brothers. Larien was young, athletically built, strikingly handsome, had an engaging smile. Noal, evidently the older by a good many years, seemed a washed-out personality—slight, stooped, colorless. Hishee was a slender blonde with slanted black eyes and a cowed look. Her voice matched the look; it was low and uncertain. Telzey went through that recording again, ignoring Hishee's words, absorbing the voice tones.

She closed the file then. "Where's the rest of it?"

"The rest of it," said Dasinger, "is officially none of the Kyth Agency's business at the moment. Hence it isn't in the agency files."

"Oh?"

"You know a place called Joca Village, near Great Alzar?"

She nodded. "I've been there."

"Larien Selk acquired an estate in the Village three months ago," Dasinger said. "It's at the northeast end, an isolated cliffside section overlooking the sea. We know Larien is there at present. And we've found out that Noal Selk was in fact kidnapped by professionals and turned over to Larien's people. The probability is that he's now in Larien's place in Joca Village. If they try to move him out of there, he'll be in our hands. But that's the only good prospect of getting him back alive we have so far. Larien has been given no reason to believe anyone is looking for his brother, or that anyone but Hishee has begun to suspect Noal is missing. That's our immediate advantage. We can't afford to give it up."

Telzey nodded, beginning to understand. Joca Village was an ultraexclusive residential area, heavily guarded. If you weren't a resident or hadn't been issued a pass by a resident, you didn't get in. Passes were carefully checked at the single entrance, had to be confirmed. Overhead screens barred an aerial approach. She said, "And you can't go to the authorities until you have him back."

"No," Dasinger said. "If we did, we'd never get him back. We might be able to pin murder on Larien Selk later, though that's by no means certain. In any case, it isn't what we're after." He hesitated, said questioningly after a moment, "Telzey?"

Telzey blinked languidly.

"Telzey—" Dasinger broke off, watching her. Wergard glanced at him. Dasinger made a quick negating motion with his hand. Wergard shifted his attention back to Telzey.

"I heard you," Telzey said some seconds later. "You have Hishee Selk here in the agency, don't you?"

Wergard looked startled. Dasinger said, "Yes, we do."

"It was her voice mainly," Telzey said. "I picked her up on that." She looked at Wergard. "Wergard can't really believe this kind of thing is real."

"I'm trying to suspend my doubts," Wergard said. "Bringing in a mind-reader wasn't my idea. But we could use one only too well here."

Dasinger said, "All right to go on now, Telzey?"

"Oh, yes," she said. "I was gone for only a moment. Now I'm making contact, and Hishee looks wide open. She's very easy!" She straightened up in her chair. "Just what do you want your mind-reader to do?"

Dasinger said to Wergard, "What Telzey means is that, having seen what Hishee Selk looks like, and having heard her voice, she gained an impression of Hishee's personality. She then sensed a similar impression around here, found a connection to the personality associated with it, and is now feeling her way into Hishee's mind. Approximately correct, Telzey?"

"Very close." For a nonpsi, Dasinger did, in fact, have a good understanding of psi processes.

"Now as to your question," he went on. "When Larien Selk bought the place in Joca Village, he had it equiped with security devices, installed by Banance Protective Systems, a very good outfit. During the past week, Banance added a few touches—mainly a Brisell pack and its handler. At the same time, the Colmer Detective Agency in Great Alzar was employed to provide round-the-clock guards, five to a shift, stationed directly at the house, behind the pack. However, we've obtained copies of the Banance security diagrams which show the setup on the grounds. And, of course, there are various ways of handling guards."

"You mean you can get into Joca Village and into the house?"

"Very likely. One of the residents is an agency client and has supplied us with Village passes. Getting in the Selk estate and into the house without alerting security presents problems, but shouldn't be too difficult. Everything is set up to do it now, two or three hours after nightfall at Joca Village. It's after we're inside the house that the matter becomes really ticklish."

Wergard said, "It's a one-shot operation. If we start it, it has to come off. We can't back away, and try again. Either Noal will be safe before his brother realizes somebody is trying to rescue him, or he'll have disappeared for good."

Telzey considered. It was easy enough to dispose of a human being instantly and tracelessly. "And you don't *know* Noal's in the house?" she said.

"No," Dasinger said. "There's a strong probability he's there. If we can't do better, we'll have to act on that probability tonight, because every hour of delay puts his life—if he's still alive—in greater danger. If he isn't there, Larien is the one person in the house who's sure to know where he is. But picking up Larien isn't likely to do Noal any good. He's bound to have taken precautions against that, and again Noal, wherever he is, will simply vanish, along with any evidence pointing to him. So we come back to the mind-reader—somebody who can tell us from Larien's mind exactly where Noal is and what we can do about it, before Larien knows we're in the house."

"Yes, I see," Telzey said. "But there're a number of things I *don't* understand here. Why does Larien—" She broke off, looked reflective a moment, nodded. "I can get that faster from Hishee now! It's all she's thinking about."

2

Larien Selk, legally and biologically Noal's junior by twenty-five years, was, in the actual chronology of events, the older brother. He'd been conceived first by three years. The parents were engaged in building up a business and didn't want to be burdened with progeny taxes. The Larien-to-be went to an embryonic suspense vault. When Noal was conceived, the family could more readily afford a child, and the mother decided she preferred giving natural birth to one.

So Noal was born. His parents had no real wish for a second child. They kept postponing a decision about the nameless embryo they'd stored away, and in the end seemed almost to have forgotten it. It wasn't until they'd died that Noal, going through old records, found a reference to his abandoned sibling. Somewhat shocked by his parents' indifference, he had Larien brought to term. When his brother grew old enough to understand the situation, Noal explained how he'd come to take his place.

Larien never forgave him. Noal, a shrewd enough man in other respects, remained unaware of the fact. He saw to it that Larien had the best of everything—very nearly whatever Larien wanted. When he came of age, Noal made him a partner in the company he'd founded and developed. Which put Larien in a position to begin moving against his brother.

Hishee was his first move. Hishee was to have married Noal. She was very young, but she was fond of him and a formal agreement wasn't far away. Then Larien turned his attention on Hishee, and the formal agreement was never reached. Hishee fell violently in love.

Noal accepted it. He loved them both; they were near the same age. But he found it necessary to detach himself from them. He waited until they married, then turned the effective management of the company over to Larien, and began traveling.

Larien set out casually to break Hishee. He did an unhurried thorough job of it, gradually, over the months, eroding her self-esteem and courage in a considered variety of ways. He brought her to heel, continued to reduce her. By the time Noal Selk came back to Cobril, Hishee was too afraid of Larien, too shaken in herself, to give her brother-in-law any indication of what had happened.

But Noal saw it. Larien had wanted him to see it, which was a mistake. Larien wasn't quite as well covered in his manipulation of the company's assets as he'd believed.

Noal, alerted to Larien's qualities, became also aware of that. He made a quiet investigation. It led him presently to the Kyth detective agency.

Then he disappeared.

Dasinger said dryly, "We'd put you on the Kyth payroll any time, Telzey! It took us some hours to extract half that information from Hishee. The rest of it checks. If Larien thinks it's safe, he'll see Noal broken completely before he dies. No doubt he's made ingenious arrangements for that. He's an ingenious young man. But the time we have for action remains narrowly limited."

"He doesn't know Hishee's gone?" Telzey asked.

"Not yet. We have that well covered. We had to take her out of the situation; she'd be in immediate danger now. But it's an additional reason for avoiding delay. If Larien begins to suspect she had courage enough left to try to save Noal, he'll destroy the evidence. He should be able to get away with it legally, and he knows it."

Telzey was silent a moment. There were some obscure old laws against witchcraft, left deliberately unchanged, very rarely applied. Aside from that, the Federation was officially unaware of the existence of psis; a psi's testimony was meaningless. Legally then, it was probably enough that Larien Selk could get away with the murder of his brother. She doubted he'd survive Noal long; the private agencies had their own cold rules. But, as Dasinger had said, that wasn't what they were after.

She said, "Why do you want to plant the telepath in the house? If he's good enough, he should be able to tap Larien's mind from somewhere outside Joca Village, though it probably would take a little longer."

Wergard said, "One of the Banance security devices is what's known technically as a psi-block. It covers the outer walls of the house. Larien shares some of the public superstitions about the prevalence of efficient mind-reading instruments. Presumably the block would also stop a human telepath."

She nodded. "Yes, they do."

"When he's outside one of his psi-blocked structures, he wears a mind shield," Wergard said. "A detachable type. If we'd known about this a little earlier, we might have had an opportunity to pick him up and relieve him if it. But it's too late now."

"Definitely too late," Dasinger agreed. "If you think you can find us a telepath who's more than a hit-and-miss operator, we'd take a chance on waiting another day, if necessary, to bring him in on it. But it would be taking a chance. If you can't get one, we'll select a different approach and move to-night."

Telzey said, "A telepath wouldn't be much good to you if Larien happens to be probe-immune. About one in eight people are."

"Seven to one are good odds in the circumstances," Da-singer said. "Very good odds. We'll risk that."

"They're better than seven to one," Telzey told him. "Probe-immunes usually don't know that's what they are, but they usually don't worry about having their minds read either. They feel safe." She rubbed her nose, frowning. "A Psychology Service psi could do the job for you, and I can try getting one. But I don't think they'll help. They won't lift a finger in ordinary crime cases."

Dasinger shook his head. "I can't risk becoming involved with them here anyway. Technically it's an illegal operation. The Kyth Agency won't be conducting it unless we come up with evidence that justified the illegality. I resigned yesterday, and Wergard and some others got fired. We'll be acting as pri-vate citizens. But that's also only a technicality, and the Ser-vice is unpredictable. I don't know what view they'd take of it. We might have them blocking us instead of helping. Can you find someone else?"

She nodded. "I can get you a telepath. Just one. The other psis I know won't touch it. They don't need the fee, and they don't want to reveal themselves—particularly not in some-thing that's illegal."

"Who's the one?" Wergard asked.

"I am, of course."

They looked at her a moment. Wergard said, "That isn't what we had in mind. We want a pro who'll take his chances for the money he's getting. We needed information from you, but no more than that."

Telzey said, "It looks like it's turned into more than that."

Wergard said to Dasinger, "We can't get her involved."

"Corvin Wergard," Telzey said.

He looked back at her. "Yes?"

"I'm not reading your thoughts," she said. "I don't have to. You've been told who I am, and that I'm sixteen years old. So I'm a child. A child who comes of a very good family and has been very carefully raised. Somebody really too nice to get shot tonight, if something goes wrong, by a Colmer guard or Joca security people, or ripped up by Brisells. Right?"

Wergard studied her a long moment. "I may have had such notions," he said then. "Perhaps I've been wrong about you."

"You've definitely been wrong about me," Telzey told him. "You didn't know enough. I've been a psi, a practicing psi, for almost a year. I can go through a human life in an hour and know more about it than the man or woman who's living it. I've gone through quite a few lives, not only human ones. I do other things that I don't talk about. I don't know what it all exactly makes me now, but I'm not a child. Of course, I *am* sixteen years old and haven't been that very long. But it might even be that sometimes people like you and Wellan Dasinger look a little like children to me. Do you understand?"

"I'm not sure," Wergard said. He shook his head. "I believe I'm beginning to."

"That's good. We should have an understanding of each other if we're to work together. The agency would save the fee, too," Telzey said. "I don't need it. Of course, there may come a time when I'll ask you to stick your neck out for something I'd like to have done."

Wergard asked Dasinger, "Has that been the arrangement?"

Dasinger nodded. "We exchange assistance in various matters." He added, "I still don't want you in this, Telzey. There will be risks. Not unreasonable ones; but our people are trained to look out for themselves in ways you're not. You're too valuable a person to be jeopardized on an operation of this kind."

"Then I can't help you help Noal Selk," she said. "I'd like to. But the only way I can do it is by going along with you tonight. It would take more time than you have to hunt around for somebody else."

Dasinger shook his head. "We'll use a different approach then. With a little luck, we can still save Noal. He isn't your problem."

"How do you know?" Telzey said. "He mightn't be if he were someone I'd only heard about. If I helped everybody I could help because I happen to be a psi, I'd have no time for anything else the rest of my life. There isn't a minute in the day I couldn't find someone somewhere who needs the kind of help I can give. I'd keep busy, wouldn't I? And, of course, everything I did still wouldn't make any real difference. There'd always be more people needing help."

"There would be, of course," Dasinger agreed.

She smiled. "It gave me a bad conscience for a while, but I decided I wasn't going to get caught in that. I'll do something, now and then. Now, here I've been in Hishee Selk's mind. I'm still in her mind. I know her, and Noal and Larien as she knows them—perhaps better than most people know the members of their family. So I can't say their problem isn't my problem. It wouldn't be true. I simply know them too well."

Dasinger nodded. "Yes, I see now."

"And I," said Wergard, "made a large mistake."

Dasinger looked at his watch. "Well, let's not waste time. The plan goes into operation in thirty minutes. Telzey, you're going high style—Joca Vollage level. Wergard, take her along, have her outfitted. Scratch Woni. We won't need her."

3

The only entry to the secluded Selk estate in Joca Village was a narrow road winding between sheer cliff walls. Two hundred yards along the road was a gate; and the gate was guarded by Selk employees.

Up this road came a great gleaming limousine, preceded by a cry of golden horns. It stopped near the gate, and Larien Selk's three guards moved forward, weapons in their hands, to instruct the intruders to turn back. But they came prepared to give the instruction in as courteous a manner as possible. It was unwise to offer unnecessary offense to people who went about in that kind of limousine.

Its doors had opened meanwhile; and, gaily and noisily, out came Wergard in a Space Admiral's resplendent and heavily decorated uniform; Dasinger with jeweled face mask, a Great Alzar dandy; Telzey, finally, slender and black-gowned, wearing intricate silver headgear. From the headgear blazed the breath-stopping beauty of two great star hyacinths, proclaiming her at once to be the pampered darling of one who looked on ordinary millionaires as such millionaires might look on the lowest of bondsmen.

Weapons most tactfully lowered, the guards attempted to explain to these people—still noisily good-natured, but dangerous in their vast arrogance and wealth and doubly unpredictable now because they were obviously high on something —that a mistake had been made, that, yes, of course, their passes must be honored, but this simply didn't happen to be a route to the estate of the Askab Odarch. In the midst of these respectful explanations, an odd paralysis and confusion came to the guards. They offered no objection when men stepped out from behind the limousine, gently took their weapons and led them toward the small building beside the gate, where Wergard already was studying the gate controls. The study was a brief one; the gate's energy barrier, reaching up to blend into the defense shield of Joca Village above, winked out of existence a minute later and the great steel frames slid silently back into the rock walls on either side. The instruments which normally announced the opening of the gate to scanners in the Selk house remained inactive.

The limousine drifted through and settled to the ground beside the road. The gate closed again, and the vehicle was out of sight. Joca Village security patrols would check this gate, as they did the gates of all Village residents, several times during the night, and leaving the limousine outside would have caused questions. Whether suspicions were aroused otherwise depended mainly on whether someone began to wonder why Larien Selk's three gate guards were men who hadn't been seen here before. Measures had been taken to meet that contingency, but they were measures Dasinger preferred not to bring into play at present. The goal was to get Telzey into the house quickly, find out where Noal Selk was, pick him up if he was here and get back out with him, with no more time lost than could be helped. Whether or not his brother came along would be determined by what they discovered. With luck in either case, they'd be out of Joca Village again, mission accomplished, before the next patrol reached the Selk estate.

Only Dasinger, Wergard, and Telzey had gone through with the limousine. They emerged from it quickly again, now in fitted dark coveralls, caps and gloves, difficult to make out in the nighttime half-dark of the cliff road, and with more sophisticated qualities which were of value to burglars seeking entry into a well-defended residence. They moved silently along the road in the thick-soled sound-absorbing boots which went with the coveralls, Wergard carrying a sack. The road led around a turn of the cliffs; and a hundred yards beyond the turn, Dasinger said, "You might give them the first blast from here."

They stopped. The rock wall on the left was lower at this point, continued to slope downward along the stretch of road ahead. Wergard opened the sack and took out a tube a foot long and about three inches in diameter. He lifted the tube, sighting along it to a point above the cliffs on the left, pressed a trigger button. Something flicked silently out of the mouth of the tube and vanished in the dark air. They went on fifty yards, stopped again, and Wergard repeated the performance. The next time they stopped, the cliff on the left had dwindled to a rocky embankment not much more than twelve feet high. Larien Selk's big house stood in its gardens beyond the embankment, not visible from here.

They stood listening.

"It's got them," Wergard said then, low-voiced. "If it hadn't, they'd be aware of us by now, and we'd hear them moving around."

"Might as well give them a third dose, to be sure," Dasinger remarked.

"Why not?" Wergard agreed. He took a third tube from the sack, adjusted its settings, squinting through the dusk, then discharged its contents up across the embankment. The copies of the diagrams briefly borrowed from the files of Banance Protective Systems had showed that beyond the fence above the embankment was the area patrolled by a dozen Brisell dogs, dependable man-killers with acute senses. The three canisters Wergard had fired into the area were designed to put them out of action. They contained a charge stunning canine olfactory centers, approximately equivalent, Telzey had gathered, to the effect which might have been achieved by combining the most violent odors obtainable in their heaviest possible concentration, and releasing the mix in a flash of time. The canine mind thus treated went into prolonged dazed shock.

"Getting anything so far?" Dasinger asked her.

She nodded. "There is a psi-blocked area around. It seems

to be where the house is. If Noal and Larien are here, they're in that area."

She'd kept bringing up impressions of both Selk brothers on the way from Orado City—things she knew about them from Hishee Selk's recalls and reflections, and from the visual and auditory recordings her own senses had registered. After they'd passed through the gate, she'd been searching mentally for anything which might relate to those impressions, blocking off her awareness of Wergard and Dasinger. There'd been occasional faint washes of human mind activities hereabouts, but they carried unfamiliar patterns. She'd fastened on the most definite of those and was developing the contact when Dasinger addressed her.

She mentioned this now, added, "It's one of the Colmer guards outside the house. Nobody's expecting trouble there. I can't tell yet what he's thinking, but nothing's worrying him."

Dasinger smiled. "Good! Keep your inner ears tuned to the boy! That could be useful. Let's move on—starting from here, as ghosts."

He reached under his collar as he spoke, abruptly became a bulkier smoky figure, features distorted though still vaguely distinguishable. There was a visual dispersion effect connected with the coverall suits, increasing with distance. Wergard and Telzey joined him in apparent insubstantiality. They went around the embankment, came to the fence.

It was more than a fence. Closely spaced along the rails topping it, twenty feet above, were concealed pickup devices which registered within the house. The diagrams had listed and described them. Now reasonable caution and the equipment in the suits of the three trespassers should give the devices nothing to register.

They moved slowly along the fence, twelve feet apart, not speaking here though they carried distorters which smothered voice tones within the distance of a few feet, until Wergard, in the lead, reached a closed gate where the road they'd been following turned through the fence. His wavering contours stopped there; and Telzey and Dasinger also stopped where they were. Wergard was the burglary expert; his job was now to get them through the gate. It was locked, of course. The relays which opened the lock were in the house, and the lock itself was a death trap for anyone attempting to tamper with it. However, nobody had seemed concerned about those details, and Telzey decided not to worry either. Wergard was doing something, but she couldn't determine what. His foggy shape blurred out a quarter of the gate. Which wasn't bothering Wergard; the effect wasn't a subjective one. Telzey could see a faint haze about herself, which moved as she did. But it didn't interfere with her vision or blur her view of herself. She looked over at the house, still more than half hidden here by intervening trees.

It was a large windowless structure. A pale glow bathed the lower section of the front wall. That came from a lit area they'd have to cross. Closer to them, on this side of the trees, the ground was shadowy, heavily dotted with sizable shrubs, through which she could make out the outlines of a high hedge. This was where the Brisell pack prowled. She thought she could distinguish something moving slowly on the ground between two shrubs. It might be one of the dogs. Otherwise there was no sign of them.

A voice suddenly said something.

Telzey didn't move. She hadn't heard those words through her ears but through the ears of her contact. He was replying now, the sound of his own voice less distinct, a heavy rumble. She blinked, pushing probes out quickly into newly accessible mind areas, orienting herself. The contact was opening up nicely. . . .

A hand tapped her shoulder. She looked up at Dasinger beside her. He indicated the gate, where Wergard had stepped back and stood waiting for them. The gate was open.

The thing she'd thought she'd seen moving occasionally on the ground between two shrub clusters was one of the Brisells. He was lying on his side as they came up, and, except for jerking his hind legs slightly, he wasn't moving just then. Two other dogs, not far from him, had been out of sight behind the shrubs. One turned in slow circles, with short, staggering steps. The other sat with drooping head, tongue lolling far down, shaking himself every few seconds. They were powerful animals with thick necks, huge heads and jaws, torsos protected by flexible corselets. None of them paid the slightest attention to the human ghost shapes.

Dasinger beckoned Telzey and Wergard to him, said softly, "They'll be no good for an hour or two. But we don't know that our business here will be over in an hour or two. We'll get their handler in the shelter now. Then it should be worth a few minutes finding the rest of the pack and putting them out till tomorrow with stun charges."

Wergard nodded; and Dasinger said to Telzey, "Stay here near those three so we don't lose you."

"All right."

She watched them hold their guns briefly to the heads of the dogs. Then the blurred shapes moved soundlessly off, becoming more apparitional with each step. In moments, she couldn't see them at all. The dogs lay unmoving now; and nothing else stirred nearby. She went back to her contact. Human thought whispers which came from other minds were reaching her from time to time, but she didn't try to develop those touches. The man she'd started working on was in charge of the Colmer Agency group and stationed near the entry of the house, directly beyond the lit area. She should get the best results here by concentrating attention on him.

His superficial thoughts could be picked up readily by now. It was the thinking of a bored, not very intelligent man, but a dangerous and well-trained one. A human Brisell. He and his group were in the second hour of an eight-hour stint of guard duty. He was looking forward to being relieved. Telzey gave the vague flow of thoughts prods here and there, turning them into new directions. She got a self-identification: his name was Sommard. He and the other Colmar guards knew nothing of what went on inside the house, and weren't interested. On arrival, they'd been admonished to constant alertness by a Mr. Costian. Sommard figured Mr. Costian for a nervous nut; the place obviously was well protected without them. But that wasn't his business, and he was doing his duty, however perfunctorily. His attention never wandered far. Two other guards stood to his right and left some fifty yards away, at the corners of the house. The remaining two were at the rear of the building where there was a service entry. . . . That checked with what the Kyth Agency had established about the defense arrangements.

There was a sudden wash of mental brightness. It steadied, and Telzey was looking out of Sommard's eyes into the wide illuminated court below the house where the estate road terminated. Keeping watch on that open area, up to the fence on the far side and the locked road gate in the fence, was his immediate responsibility. If anyone not previously authorized by Mr. Costian to be there appeared in the court, there'd be no challenge. He'd give his companions and the people in the house a silent alert, and shoot the intruder. Of course, no one would appear there! He yawned.

Telzey let the view of the court go, made some preparations, reduced contact, and glanced at her watch. It had been four and a half minutes since the Kyth men left her. She began looking about for them, presently saw a haziness some twenty feet away, condensing slightly and separating into two shapes as it drew closer. A genuine pair of ghosts couldn't have moved more quietly. "The section's taken care of," Dasinger was saying then. "Anything to report?"

Telzey told them what she'd learned. Dasinger nodded. "Costian's been Larien Selk's underworld contact on Orado. It's probable that the pros delivered Noal to him." He scratched his chin. "Now what's the best way to take the agency guards out gently? We have no dispute with Colmer."

Wergard said, "Going through the gate's still possible, but it'll call for fast moving once we're through or we'd risk disturbance. The long way around past the cliffs seems safer to me."

Telzey shook her head.

"That won't be necessary," she said.

Sommard presently shut his eyes for no particular reason except that he felt like it. The road gate across the court opened slightly, stayed open a few seconds, closed quietly again. Sommard then roused himself, looked briskly about. He glanced at his two colleagues, stationed at the corners of the house on either side of him. They stood unmoving, as bored as he was. All was well. He scratched his chest, yawned again.

Thirty feet from him, invisible as far as he was concerned, Telzey settled herself on the low balustrade above the court, looked at him, reached back into his mind. She waited. Something like a minute passed. The guard at the corner to Sommard's left took two stumbling steps to the side and fell backward.

Sommard's awareness blanked out in the same instant. His knees buckled; he slid down along the wall against which he had been leaning, went over on his side and lay still.

Telzey looked around at the guard at the other house corner. He was down and out, too, and Wergard and Dasinger were now on their way along the sides of the house to take care of the two guards at the rear. She stood up and went over to Sommard. What she'd done to him was a little more complicated than using a stun gun, a good deal gentler than a stun gun's jolt. The overall effect, however, was the same. He'd go on sleeping quietly till morning.

She stayed beside him to make it easier for Dasinger to find her when he came to take her to the back of the house. There was an entry there which led to the servants' quarters below ground level. They would use that way to get into the house. There should be only three men in the servants' quarters tonight—Larien Selk's second gate guard team. They might be asleep at present. The estate's normal staff had been trasferred to other properties during the past week. In the upper house were Costian, Larien Selk, probably Noal Selk, and two technicians who kept alternate watch on the instruments of the protective system. That was all.

Getting into the house wasn't likely to be much of a problem now. But the night's work might have only begun.

4

"I'm getting traces of Larien," Telzey said.

"And Noal?" Dasinger asked.

"I'm not sure. There was something for a moment—but—" Her voice trailed off unsteadily.

"Take your time." Dasinger, leaning against a table ten feet away, watching her in the dim glow of a ceiling light, had spoken quietly. They'd turned off the visual distorters; the ghost haze brought few advantages indoors. Wergard had found the three off-duty gate guards asleep, left them sleeping more soundly. He'd gone off again about some other matter. Telzey and Dasinger were to stay on the underground level until she'd made her contacts, established what the situation here was.

She leaned back in her chair, closed her eyes, sighed. There was silence then. Dasinger didn't stir. Telzey's face was pale, intent. After a while, her breathing grew ragged. Her lips twisted slowly. It might have been a laborious mouthing of words heard in her mind. Her fingers plucked fitfully at the material of the coveralls. Then she grew quiet. Wergard returned soundlessly, remained standing outside the door.

Telzey opened her eyes, looked at Dasinger and away from him, straightened up in the chair, and passed her tongue over her lips.

"It's no use," she said in a flat, drained voice.

"You couldn't contact Noal?"

She shook her head. "Perhaps I could. I don't know. You'll have to get the psi block shut off, and I'll try. He's not in the house." She began crying suddenly, stopped as suddenly. A valve had opened; had been twisted shut. "But we can't help him," she said. "He's dying."

"Where is he?"

"In the sea."

"In the sea? Go ahead."

She shrugged. "That's it! In the sea, more or less east of Joca Village. It might be a hundred miles from here, or two thousand. I don't know; nobody knows. Larien didn't want anybody to know, not even himself."

Wergard had come into the room. She looked over at him, back at Dasinger. "It's a bubble for deep water work. Something the Selks made on Cobril. Marine equipment. Larien had it brought in from Cobril. This one has no operating controls. It was just dropped off, somewhere."

An automated carrier had been dispatched, set on random course. For eight hours it moved about the sea east of the mainland; then it disintegrated and sank. At some randomly selected moment during those eight hours, relays had closed, and the bubble containing Noal Selk began drifting down through the sea.

She told them that.

Dasinger said. "You said he's dying. . . ."

She nodded. "He's being eaten. Some organism—it tries to keep the animals it feeds on alive as long as it can. It's very careful . . . I don't know what it is."

"I know what it is," Dasinger said. "When was it injected?"

"Two days ago."

Dasinger looked at Wergard. Wergard shrugged, said, "You might find something still clinically alive in the bubble five days from now. If you want to save Noal Selk, you'd better do it in hours."

"It's worth trying!" Dasinger turned to Telzey. "Telzey, what arrangements has Larien made in case the thing got away from him?"

"It isn't getting away from him," she said. "The bubble's got nondetectable coating. And if somebody tried to open it, it would blow up. There's a switch in the house that will blow it up any time. Larien's sitting two feet from the switch right now. But he can't touch it."

"Why not?" Wergard asked.

Telzey glanced at him. "He can't move. He can't even think. Not till I let him again."

Dasinger said, "The destruct switch isn't good enough. Isn't there something else in the house, something material, we can use immediately as evidence of criminal purpose?"

Telzey's eyes widened. "Evidence?" For a moment, she seemed about to laugh. "Goodness, yes, Dasinger! There's all the evidence in the world. He's got Noal on screen, two-way contact. He was talking to Noal when I started to pick him up. That's why—"

"Anyone besides Costian and the two techs around?" Dasinger asked Wergard.

"No."

"Put them away somewhere," Dasinger said. "Telzey and I will be with Larien Selk."

They weren't going to find the bubble. And if some accident had revealed its location, they wouldn't have got Noal Selk out of it alive.

They hadn't given up. Dasinger was speaking to the Kyth Agency by pocket transmitter within a minute after he'd entered Larien's suite with Telzey, and the agency promptly unsheathed its claws. Operators, who'd come drifting into Joca Village during the evening, showing valid passes, converged at the entry to the Selk estate, set up some lethal equipment, and informed Village Security the section was sealed. Village Security took a long, thoughtful look at what confronted it in the gate road, and decided to wait for developments.

Dasinger remained busy with the transmitter, while Wergard recorded what Larien's two-way screen showed. Telzey, only half following the talk, spoke only when Dasinger asked questions. She reported patiently then what he wanted to know, information she drew without much difficulty from Larien's paralyzed mind—the type of nondetectable material coating the deep water device; who had applied it; the name of the Cobril firm which installed the detonating system. They were attacking the problem from every possible angle, getting the help of researchers from around the planet. On Cobril, there was related activity by now. Authorities who would be involved in a sea search here had been alerted, were prepared to act if called on. The Kyth Agency had plenty of pull and was using it.

The fact remained that Larien Selk had considered the possibilities. It had taken careful investigation, but no special knowledge. He'd wanted a nondetectable coating material and a tamper-proof self-destruct system for his deep water device. Both were available; and that was that. Larien had accomplished his final purpose. The brother who'd cheated him out of his birthright, for whom he'd been left in a vault, ignored forgotten, incomplete, had been detached from humanity and enclosed in another vault where he was now being reduced piecemeal, and from which he would never emerge. As the minutes passed, it became increasingly clear that what Dasinger needed to change the situation was an on-the-spot scientific miracle. Nothing suggested there were miracles forthcoming. Lacking that, they could watch Noal Selk die, or, if they chose, speed his death.

Telzey bit at her lip, gaze fastened on Larien, who lay on a couch a dozen feet from her. They'd secured his hands behind his back, which wasn't necessary; she'd left her controls on him, and he was caught in unawareness which would end when she let it end. That strong, vital organism was helpless now, along with the mind that had wasted itself in calculating hatred for so many years.

There was something here she hadn't wanted to see. . . .

A psi mentality needed strong shutoffs. It had them, developed them quickly, or collapsed into incoherence. The flow of energies which reached nonpsis in insignificant tricklings, must be channeled, directed, employed—or sealed away. Shutoffs were necessary. But they could be misapplied. Too easily, too thoroughly, by a mind that had learned to make purposeful use of them.

There was something she'd blocked out of awareness not

long ago. For a while, she'd succeeded in forgetting she'd done it. She knew now that she had done it, but it was difficult to hold her attention on the fact. Her mind drew back from such thoughts, kept sliding away, trying to distract itself, trying to blur the act in renewed forgetfulness.

She didn't want to find out what it was she'd shut away. By that, she knew it was no small matter. There was fear involved.

Of what was she afraid?

She glanced uneasily over at the screen showing the brightly lit metallic interior of the bubble. Wergard stood before it, working occasionally at his recordings. She hadn't looked at the screen for more than a few seconds since coming into the room. It could be turned to a dozen views, showing the same object from different angles and distances. The object was a human body which wasn't quite paralyzed because it sometimes stirred jerkily, and its head moved. The eyes were sometimes open, sometimes shut. It looked unevenly shrunken, partly defleshed by what seemed a random process, skin lying loosely on bone here and there, inches from the swell of muscle. However, the process wasn't a random one; the alien organism within the body patched up systematically behind itself as it made its selective harvest. Outside tubes were attached to the host. The body wouldn't die of dehydration or starvation; it was being nourished. It would die when not enough of it was left to bind life to itself, or earlier if the feeding organism misjudged what it was doing. Dasinger had said its instincts were less reliable with humans because they weren't among its natural food animals.

Or Noal Selk would die when it was decided he couldn't be saved, and somebody's hand reached for the destruct switch.

In any case, he would die. What the screen showed were the beginnings of his death, whatever turn it took in the end. There was no reason for her to watch that. Noal, lost in the dark sea, in his small bright-lit tomb unknown miles from here, was beyond her help, beyond all help now.

Her eyes shifted back to Larien. It happened, she decided, at some point after she'd moved into his mind, discovered what he had done, and, shocked, was casting about for further information, for ways to undo this atrocity. Almost now, but not quite, she could remember the line of reflections she'd followed, increasingly disturbed reflections they seemed to be.

Then—then she'd been past that point. Something flashed up, some horrid awareness; instantly she'd buried it, sealed it away, sealed away that entire area of recall.

She shook her head slightly. It remained buried! She remembered doing it now, and she wouldn't forget that again. But she didn't remember what she had buried, or why. Perhaps if she began searching in Larien Selk's mind . . .

At the screen, Wergard exclaimed something. Telzey looked up quickly. Dasinger had turned away from the table where he'd been sitting, was starting toward the screen. Sounds began to come from the screen. She felt the blood drain from her face.

Something was howling in her mind—wordless expression of a terrible need. It went on for seconds, weakened abruptly and was gone. Other things remained.

She stood up, walked unsteadily to the screen. The two men glanced around as she came up. An enlarged view of Noal Selk's head filled the screen. There were indications that the feeder had been selectively at work here, too; but there wasn't much change in the features. The eyes were wide open, staring up past the pickup. The mouth was lax and trembling; only wet, shaky breathing sounds came from it now.

Wergard said, "For some moments, he seemed fully conscious. He seemed to see us. He—well, the speaking apparatus isn't essential to life, of course. Most of that may be gone. But I think he was trying to speak to us."

Telzey, standing between them, looking at the screen, said, "He saw you. He was trying to ask you to kill him. Larien let him know it could be done any time."

Dasinger said carefully, "You *know* he was trying to ask us to kill him?"

"Yes, I know," Telzey said. "Be quiet, Dasinger. I have to think now."

She blinked slowly at the screen. Her diaphragm made a sudden, violent contraction as a pain surge reached her. Pain shutoff went on; the feeling dimmed. Full contact here.

Her mouth twisted. She hadn't wanted it! Not after what she'd learned. That was what she hadn't allowed to come into consciousness. She'd told herself it wasn't possible to reach Noal where he was, even after they'd shut off the psi block in the walls of the house. She'd convinced herself it was impossible. But she'd made the contact, and it had developed, perhaps as much through Noal's frenzied need as through anything she'd done; and now she'd been blazingly close to his mind and body torment—

She brushed her hand slowly over her forehead. She felt clammy with sweat.

"Telzey, is something wrong with you?" Dasinger asked.

She looked up at their watchful faces.

"No, not really. Dasinger, you know you can't save him, don't you?"

His expression didn't change. "I suppose I do," he acknowledged. "I suppose we all do. But we'll have to go on trying for a while, before we simply put him to death."

She nodded, eyes absent. "There's something I can try," she told them. "I didn't think of it before."

"Something *you* can try?" Wergard said, astonished. His head indicated the screen. "To save him *there?*"

"Yes. Perhaps."

Dasinger cleared his throat. "I don't see . . . what do you have in mind?"

She shook her head. "I can't explain that. It's psi. I'll try to explain as I go along, but I probably won't be able to explain much. It may work, that's all. I've done something like it before."

"But you can't—" Wergard broke off, was silent.

Dasinger said, "You know what you're doing?"

"Yes, I know." Telzey looked up at them again. "You mustn't let anyone in here. There musn't be any disturbance or interference, or everything might go wrong. And it will take time. I don't know how much time."

Neither of them said anything for some seconds. Then Dasinger nodded slowly.

"Whatever it is," he said, "you'll have all the time you need. Nobody will come in here. Nobody will be allowed on the estate before you've finished and give the word."

Telzey nodded. "Then this is what we'll have to do."

5

She had done something like this, or something nearly like this, before. . . .

Here and there was a psi mind with whom one could exchange the ultimate compliment of using no mental safeguards, none whatever. It was with one of those rare, relaxing companions that she'd done almost what she'd be doing now. The notion had come up in the course of a psi practice session. One was in Orado City, one at the tip of the Southern Mainland at the time. They'd got together at the thought level, and were trying out various things, improving techniques and methods.

"I'll lend you what *I* see if you'll lend me what *you* see," one of them had said.

That was easy enough. Each looked suddenly at what the other had looked at a moment ago. It wasn't the same as tapping the sensory impressions of a controlled mind. Small sections of individual awareness, of personality, appeared to have shifted from body to body.

It went on from there. Soon each was using the other's muscles, breathing with the other's lungs, speaking wth the other's voice. They'd got caught up in it, and more subtle transfers continued in a swift double flow, unchecked: likes and dislikes, acquired knowledge, emotional patterns. Memories disintegrated here, built up there; vanished, were newly complete—and now quite different memories. Only the awareness of self remained—that probably couldn't be exchanged, or could it?

Then: "Shall we?"

They'd hesitated, looking at each other, with a quarter of the globe between them, each seeing the other clearly, in their exchanged bodies, exchanged personalities. One threadlike link was left for each to sever, and each would become the other, with no connection then to what she had been.

"Of course, we can change right back—"

Yes, but could they? Could they? Something would be different, would have shifted; they would be in some other and unknown pattern—and suddenly, quickly, they were sliding past each other again, memories, senses, controls, personality particles, swirling by in a giddy two-way stream, reassembling, restoring themselves, each to what was truly hers. They were laughing, but a little breathlessly, really a little frightened now by what they'd almost done.

They'd never tried it again. They'd talked about it. They were almost certain it could be done, oh, quite safely! They'd be two telepaths still, two psis. It should be a perfectly simple matter to reverse the process at any time.

It should be. But even to those who were psis, and in psi, much more remained unknown about psi than was known. Anyone who gained any awareness at all understood there were limits beyond which one couldn't go, or didn't try to go. Limits beyond which things went oddly wrong.

The question was whether they would have passed such a limit in detaching themselves from their personality, acquiring that of another. It remained unanswered.

What she had in mind now was less drastic in one respect, seemed more so in another. She would find out whether she could do it. She didn't know what the final result would be if she couldn't.

She dissolved her contact with Noal. It would be a distraction, and she could restore it later.

Larien Selk was fastened securely to his couch. Dasinger and Wergard then fastened Telzey as securely to the armchair in which she sat. She'd told them there might be a good deal of commotion here presently, produced both by herself and by Larien. It would be a meaningless commotion, something to be ignored. They wouldn't know what they were doing. They had to be tied down so they wouldn't get hurt.

The two men asked no questions. She reached into a section of her brain, touched it with paralysis, slid to Larien Selk's mind. In his brain, too, a selected small section went numb. Then the controls she'd placed on him were flicked away.

He woke up. He had to be awake and aware for much of this, or her work would be immeasurably, perhaps impossibly, increased. But his wakefulness did result in considerable com-

motion, though much less than there would have been if
Larien had been able to use his voice—or, by and by, Telzey's. She'd silenced both for the time being. He couldn't do
more than go through the motions of screaming. Nor could
he move around much, though he tried very hard.

For Larien, it was a terrifying situation. One moment, he'd
been sitting before the screen, considering whether to nudge the
console button which would cause a stimulant to be injected
into Noal and bring him back to consciousness again for an
hour or two. He enjoyed talking to Noal.

Then, with no discernible lapse in time, he sensed he was lying on his back, arms and legs stretched out, tied down. Simultaneously, however, he looked up from some point in mid-
air at two tense-faced men who stood between him and the
screen that peered into Noal's bubble.

Larien concluded he'd gone insane. In the next few minutes, he nearly did. Telzey was working rapidly. It wasn't
nearly as easy work as it had been with a cooperating psi; but
Larien lacked the understanding and ability to interfere with
her, as a psi who wasn't cooperating would have done. There
was, of course, no question of a complete personality exchange here. But point by point, sense by sense, function by
function, she was detaching Larien from all conscious contacts with his body. His bewildered attempts to retain each
contact brought him into a corresponding one with hers—and
that particular exchange had been made.

The process was swift. It was Larien's body that struggled
violently at first, tried to scream, strained against its fastenings. Telzey's remained almost quiescent. Then both twisted
about. Then his, by degrees, relaxed. The other body continued to twist and tug, eyes staring, mouth working desperately.

Telzey surveyed what had been done, decided enough had
been done at this level. Her personality, her consciousness,
were grafted to the body of Larien Selk. His consciousness
was grafted to her body. The unconscious flows had followed
the conscious ones.

She sealed the access routes to memory storage in the Telzey brain. The mind retained memory without the body's help
for a while. For how long a while was something she hadn't
yet established.

Time for the next step. She withdrew her contact with
Larien's mind, dissolved it. Then she cut her last mind links to

her body. It vanished from her awareness. She lay in Larien Selk's body, breathing with its lungs. She cleared its throat, lifted the paralysis she'd placed on the use of its voice.

"Dasinger!" the voice said hoarsely. "Wergard!"

Footsteps came hurrying over.

"Yes, *he's* over *there.* I'm here . . . for now. I wanted you to understand so you wouldn't worry too much."

They didn't say anything, but their faces didn't look reassured. Telzey added, "I've got his—its voice cut off. Over there, I mean."

What else should she tell them? She couldn't think of anything; and she had a driving impatience now to get on with this horrid business, to get it done, if she could get it done. To be able to tell herself it was over.

"It'll be a while before I can talk to you again," Larien Selk's voice told Wergard and Dasinger.

Then they vanished from her sight. Larien's eyes—no longer in use—closed. Telzey had gone back to work. Clearing the traces of Larien's memories and reaction patterns from his brain took time because she was very thorough and careful about it. She wanted none of that left; neither did she want to damage the brain. The marks of occupancy faded gradually, cleaned out, erased, delicately annihilated; and presently she'd finished. She sent out a search thought then to recontact the mind of Noal Selk in the brightly-lit hell of his bubble, picked up the pattern almost at once, and moved over into his mind.

He was unconscious, but something else here was conscious in a dim and limited way. Telzey turned her attention briefly to the organism which had been implanted in Noal. A psi creature, as she'd thought. The ability to differentiate so precisely between what was and was not immediately fatal to a creature not ordinarily its prey had implied the use of psi. The organism wasn't cruel; it had no concept of cruelty. It was making a thrifty use of the food supply available to it, following its life purpose.

She eased into the body awareness from which Noal had withdrawn, dimming the pain sensations which flared up in her. It was immediately obvious that very extensive damage had been done. But a kind of functional balance lingered in what was left. The body lived as a body.

And the mind still lived as a mind, sustaining itself by turning away from the terrible realities about it as often as Noal could escape from pain into unconsciousness. She considered that mind, shifting about it and through it, knowing she was confronting the difficulty she'd expected. Noal wouldn't cling to this body; in intention, he already was detached from it. But that was the problem. He was trying, in effect, to become disembodied and remain that way.

He had a strong motivation. She should be able to modify it, nullify it eventually; but it seemed dangerous to tamper with Noal any more than she could help. There wasn't enough left of him, physically or mentally, for that. He had to want to attach himself fully and consciously to a body again, or this wasn't going to work. She could arouse him, bring him awake . . .

He would resist it, she thought.

But she might give him something he wouldn't resist.

Noal dreamed.

It was a relaxed dream, universes away from pain, fear, savage treachery. He remembered nothing of Larien. He was on Cobril, walking along with a firm, quick stride in warm sunlight. He was agreeably aware of the strength and health of his body.

Something tugged at him.

Vision blurred startlingly. Sound faded. The knowledge came that the thing that tugged at him was trying to drag him wholly away from his senses, out of himself, into unfeeling nothingness.

Terrified, he fought to retain sight and sound, to cling to his body.

Telzey kept plucking him away, taking his place progressively in the still functional wreckage left by the organism, barring him more and more from it. But simultaneously she made corresponding physical anchorages available for him elsewhere; and Noal, still dreaming, not knowing the difference, clung to each point gained with frantic determination. She had all the cooperation she could use. The transfer seemed accomplished in moments.

She told him soothingly then to go on sleeping, go on dreaming pleasantly. Presently, agitations subsiding, he was doing it.

And Telzey opened Noal Selk's gummily inflamed and

bloodshot eyes with difficulty, looked out into the metallic glittering of the bubble, closed the eyes again. She was very much here—too much so. Her pain shutoffs were operating as far as she could allow them to operate without hampering other activities, but it wasn't enough. A sudden fresh set of twinges gave her a thought then; and she put the busy psi organism to sleep. At least, that part of it shouldn't get any worse.

But she'd have to stay here a while. In this body's brain was the physical storehouse of Noal's memories, the basis of his personality. It was a vast mass of material; getting it all transferred in exact detail to the brain she'd cleared out to receive it was out of the question. It probably could be done, but it would take hours. She didn't have hours to spare.

The essentials, however, that which made Noal what he was, should be transplanted in exact detail. She started doing it. It wasn't difficult work. She'd doctored memories before this, and it was essentially the same process.

It was simply a question of how much she could get done before she had to stop. The physical discomforts that kept filtering into her awareness weren't too serious a distraction. But there was something else that frightened her—an occasional sense of vagueness about herself, a feeling as if she might be growing flimsy, shadowy. It always passed quickly, but it seemed a warning that too much time was passing, perhaps already had passed, since she'd cut herself off from her own brain and body and the physical basis of memory and personality.

She paused finally. It should do. It would have to do. Her mind could absorb the remaining pertinent contents of this body's brain in a few minutes, retain it until she had an opportunity to feed back to Noal whatever else he might need. It would be secondhand memory, neither exact nor complete. But he wouldn't be aware of the difference, and no one who had known him would be able to tell there was a difference. She couldn't risk further delay. There was a sense of something that had been in balance beginning to shift dangerously, though she didn't yet know what it was.

She began the absorption process. Completed it. Went drifting slowly off, then through nothing, through nowhere. . . . Peered out presently again through puzzled sore eyes into the gleaming of the bubble.

Hot terror jolted through her—

"Dasinger!"

Dasinger turned from the couch on which the Larien body lay, came quickly across the room. "Yes?"

Wergard indicated the other figure in the armchair.

"This one seems to be coming awake again!"

Dasinger looked at the figure. It was slumped back as far as the padded fastenings which held its arms clamped against the sides of the chair permitted. The head lolled to the left, eyes slitted, blood-smeared mouth half open. "What makes you think so?" he asked.

The figure's shoulders jerked briefly almost as he spoke.

"That," Wergard said. "It's begun to stir."

They watched, but the figure remained quiet now. Wergard looked at the screen. "Some slight change there, too!" he remarked. "Its eyes were open for a while. A minute ago, they closed."

"Coinciding with the first indication of activity here?" Dasinger asked.

"Very nearly. What about the one on the couch?"

Dasinger shrugged. "Snoring! Seems to smile now and then. Nobody could be more obviously asleep."

Wergard said, after a moment, "So it must be between these two now?"

"If she's been doing what we think, it should be. . . . There!"

The figure in the chair sucked in a hissing breath, head slamming up against the back rest. The neck arched, strained, tendons protruding like tight-drawn wires. Dasinger moved quickly. One hand clamped about the jaw; the other gripped the top of the skull. "Get something back in her mouth!"

Wergard already was there with a folded wet piece of cloth, wedged it in between bared teeth, jerked his fingers back with a grunt of pain. Dasinger moved his thumb up, holding the cloth in place. The figure was in spasmodic violent motion now, dragging against the fastenings. Wergard placed his palms above its knees, pressed down hard, felt himself still being shifted about. He heard shuddering gasps, glanced up once and saw blue eyes glaring unfocused in the contorted face.

"Beginning to subside!" Dasinger said then.

Wergard didn't reply. The legs he was holding down had relaxed, gone limp, a moment before. Howling sounds came from the screen, turned into a strangled choking, went silent. He straightened, saw Dasinger take the cloth from Telzey's mouth. She looked at them in turn, moved her puffed lips, grimaced uncomfortably.

"You put your teeth through your lower lip a while ago," Dasinger explained. He added, "That wasn't you, I suppose. You *are* back with us finally, aren't you?"

She was still breathing raggedly. She whispered, "Not quite . . . almost. Moments!"

Animal sounds blared from the screen again. Their heads turned toward it. Wergard went over, cut off the noise, looked at the twisting face that had belonged to Noal Selk. He came back then and helped Dasinger free Telzey from the chair. She sat up and touched her mouth tentatively, reminding Wergard of his bitten finger. He looked at it.

Telzey followed his glance. "Did I do that, too?"

"Somebody did," Wergard said shortly. He reached for one of the cloths they'd used to keep her mouth propped open, wrapped it around the double gash. "How do you feel, Telzey?"

She shifted her shoulders, moved her legs. "Sore," she said. "Very sore. But I don't seem to have pulled anything."

"You're back all the way?"

She drew a long breath. "Yes."

Wergard nodded. "Then let's get this straight. Over there on the couch, asleep—that's now Noal Selk?"

"Yes," Telzey said. "I'll have to do a little more work on him because he doesn't have all his memory yet. But it's Noal —in everything that counts, anyway."

"He doesn't have all his memory yet," Wergard repeated. "But it's Noal!" He stared at her. "All right. And you're you again." He jerked his thumb at the screen. "So the one who's down in the bubble now is Larien Selk?"

She nodded.

"Well—" Wergard shrugged. "I was watching it," he said. He looked at Dasinger. "It happened, that's all!"

He went to the screen console, unlocked the destruct switch, and turned it over. The screen went blank.

The three of them remained silent for some seconds then,

considering the same thought. Wergard finally voiced it. "This is going to take a remarkable amount of explaining!"

"I guess it will," Telzey said. "But we won't have to do it."

"Eh?" said Dasinger.

"I know some experts," she told him. She climbed stiffly out of the chair. "I'd better get to work on Noal now, so we'll have that out of the way."

The Operator on Duty at the Psychology Service Center in Orado City lifted his eyebrows when he saw Telzey walking toward his desk in the Entry Hall. They'd met before. He pretended not to notice her then until she stopped before the desk.

He looked up. "Oh, it's you," he said indifferently.

"Yes, it's me," said Telzey. They regarded each other with marked lack of approval.

"Specifically," asked the Operator, "why are you here? I'll take it for granted it has to do with your general penchant for getting into trouble."

"I wouldn't call it that," Telzey said. "I may have broken a few Federation laws last night, but that's beside the point. I'm here to see Klayung. Where do I find him?"

The Operator on Duty leaned back in his chair and laced his fingers.

"Klayung's rather busy," he remarked. "In any case, before we bother him you might explain the matter of breaking a few Federation laws. We're not in that much of a hurry, are we?"

Telzey considered him reflectively.

"I've had a sort of rough night," she said then. "So, yes— we're in exactly that much of a hurry. Unless your shields are a good deal more solid now than they were last time."

His eyelids flickered. "You wouldn't be foolish enough to—"

"I'll count to two," Telzey said. "One."

Klayung presently laid Telzey's report sheets down again, sat scratching his chin. His old eyes were thoughtful. "Where is he at present?" he asked.

"Outside the Center, in a Kyth ambulance," Telzey told him. "We brought Hishee along, too. Asleep, of course."

Klayung nodded. "Yes, she should have almost equally careful treatment. This is a difficult case."

"You can handle it?" Telzey asked.

"Oh, yes, we can handle it. We'll handle everything. We'll have to now. This could have been a really terrible breach of secrecy, Telzey! We can't have miracles, you know!"

"Yes, I know," Telzey said. "Of course, the Kyth people are all right."

"Yes, they're all right. But otherwise—"

"Well, I know it's going to be a lot of trouble for you," she said. "And I'm sorry I caused it. But there really wasn't anything else I could do."

"No, it seems there really wasn't," Klayung agreed. "Nevertheless—well, that's something I wouldn't recommend you try very frequently!"

Telzey was silent a moment.

"I'm not sure I'd try it again for any reason," she admitted. "At the end there, I nearly didn't get back."

Klayung nodded. "There was a distinct possibility you wouldn't get back."

"Were you thinking of having Noal go on as Noal?" Telzey inquired.

"That should be the simplest approach," Klayung said. "We'll see what the Makeup Department says. I doubt it would involve excessive structural modifications. . . . You don't agree?"

Telzey said, "Oh, it would be simplest, all right. But—well, you see, Noal was just nothing physically. He's got a great body now. It would be a shame to turn him back to being a nothing again."

Klayung looked at her a moment.

"Those two have had a very bad time," Telzey continued. "Due to Larien. It seems sort of fair, doesn't it?"

"If he's to become Larien Selk officially," Klayung remarked, "there'll be a great many more complications to straighten out."

"Yes, I realize that."

"Besides," Klayung went on, "neither Noal nor Hishee might want him to look in the least like Larien."

"Well, they wouldn't now, of course," Telzey agreed. "But after your therapists have cleared up all the bad things Larien's done to them, it might be a different matter."

Klayung's sigh was almost imperceptible. "All right. Supposing we get the emotional and mental difficulties resolved first, and then let the pricinpals decide for themselves in what guise Noal is to resume his existence. Would that be satisfactory?"

Telzey smiled. "Thanks, Klayung!" she said. "Yes, very satisfactory!"

Compulsion

1

There'd been a dinner party at the Amberdon town house in Orado City that night. Telzey was home for the weekend but hadn't attended the party. Graduation exams weren't far away, and she'd decided she preferred to get in additional study time. It was mainly a political dinner anyway; she'd been at enough of those.

Most of the guests had left by now. Four of them still sat in the room below her balcony alcove with Gilas and Jessamine, her parents. They'd all strolled in together a while ago for drinks and conversation, not knowing someone was on the balcony. The talk was about Overgovernment business, some of it, from the scraps Telzey absently picked up, fairly top-secret stuff. She wasn't interested until a man named Orsler started sounding off on something about which he was evidently very much annoyed. It had to do with the activities of a young woman named Argee.

Telzey started listening then because she disliked Orsler. He was an undersecretary in Conservation, head of a subdepartment dealing with uncolonized and unclaimed worlds and the life-forms native to them. Telzey had scouted around in his mind on another occasion and discovered that those remote, unsuspecting life-forms had a dubious champion in Orsler. He was using his position to help along major exploitation schemes, from which he would benefit substantially in roundabout ways. She'd decided that if nobody had done anything about it by the time the schemes ripened, she would. She gave the Overgovernment a little quiet assistance of that kind now and then. But the time in question was still several months away.

Meanwhile, anything that vexed Orsler should make enjoyable hearing. So she listened.

The group below evidently was familiar with the subject. There was a treelike creature, recently discovered somewhere, which was dangerous to human beings. Orsler's department had it tentatively classified as "noxious vermin," which meant it could be dealt with in any manner short of complete extermination. Miss Argee, whose first name was Trigger, had learned about this; and though she lacked, as Orsler pointed out bitterly, official status of any kind, she'd succeeded in having the classification changed to "quarantined, pending investigation," which meant Orsler's department could do nothing about the pseudotrees until whatever investigations were involved had been concluded.

"The girl is simply impossible!" Orsler stated. "She doesn't seem to have the slightest understanding of the enormous expense involved in keeping a planet under dependable quarantine—let alone three of them!"

"She's aware of the expense factor," said another guest, whose voice Telzey recognized as that of a Federation Admiral who'd attended Amberdon dinners before. "In fact, she spent some time going over it with me. I found she had a good grasp of logistics. It seems she's served on a Precol world and has been on several long-range expeditions where that knowledge was put to use."

"So she's annoyed you, too!" said Orsler. "If any citizen who happens—"

"I wasn't annoyed," the Federation Admiral interrupted quietly. "I rather enjoyed her visit."

There was a pause. Then Orsler said, "It's amazing that such an insignificant matter could have been carried as far as the Hace Committee! But at least that will put a prompt end to Argee's fantastic notions. She's a Siren addict, of course, and should be institutionalized in her own interest."

Federation Councilwoman Jessamine Amberdon, who served in the Hace Ethics Committee, said pleasantly, "I'd prefer to think you're not being vindictive, Orsler."

"I?" Orsler laughed. "Of course not!"

"Then," said Jessamine, "you'll be pleased to know that the Committee is handling this as it handles all matters properly brought before it. It will await the outcome of the current investigations before it forms a conclusion. And you needn't be concerned about Miss Argee's health. We have it on good authority that while she was at one time seriously addicted to the Sirens, she's now free of such problems. Her present interest in them, in other words, is not motivated by addiction."

Orsler evidently didn't choose to reply, and the talk turned to other subjects. Regrettably, from Telzey's point of view, Orsler had found no support, and had been well squelched by Jessamine, which she liked. But now she was intrigued. Treelike Sirens which addicted people and rated a hearing in the Ethics Committee were something new.

She could ask Jessamine about it later, but she'd have to admit to eavesdropping then, which her mother would consider not quite the right thing to have done. Besides, one of the minds down there could tell her. And having been in Orsler's mind before, reentry would be a simple matter—

Unless there happened to be a Guardian Angel around. Frequently enough, they hovered about people in upper government levels, for one reason or another. She'd picked up no trace of their presence tonight, but they were rather good at remaining unnoticed.

Well, she'd find out. She dropped an entry probe casually toward Orsler.

And right enough:

"Telzey Amberdon, you stop that!"

It was a brisk, prim thought-form, carrying distinct overtones of the personality producing it. She knew this particular Guardian Angel, or Psychology Service psi operator, who probably was in a parked aircar within a block or two of the Amberdon house—a hard-working, no-nonsense little man with whom she'd skirmished before. He was no match for her; but he could get assistance in a hurry. She didn't complete the probe.

"Why?" she asked innocently. "You're not interested in Orsler, are you?"

"He's precisely the one in whom I'm interested!"

"You surprise me," said Telzey. "Orsler's a perfect creep."

"I won't argue with that description of him. But it's beside the point."

"A little mental overhauling wouldn't hurt him," Telzey pointed out. "He's no asset to the Federation as he is."

"Undersecretary Orsler," the Angel told her sternly, "is not to be tampered with! He has a function to perform of which he isn't aware. What happens after he's performed it is another matter—but certainly no business of yours."

So they knew of Orsler's planetary exploitation plans and would handle it in their way. Good enough!

"All right," Telzey said amiably. "I have no intention of tampering with him, actually. I only wanted to find out what he knows about those Sirens they were talking about."

A pause. "Information about the pseudotrees is classified," said the Angel. "But I suppose that technicality means little to you."

"Very little," Telzey agreed.

"Then I suggest that your mother knows more about the subject than anyone else in the room."

Telzey shrugged mentally. "I don't snoop in Jessamine's mind. You know that."

A longer pause. "You're really interested only in the Sirens?" asked the Angel.

"And Trigger Argee."

"Very well. I can get you a report on the former."

"How soon?"

"It will be in your telewriter by the time you reach your room. As for Miss Argee, we might have a file on her, but you can hardly expect us to violate her privacy to satisfy your curiosity."

"I wouldn't ask you to violate anyone's privacy," Telzey said. "All I'd like is her background, what kind of person she is—the general sort of thing I could get from a good detective agency tomorrow."

"I'll have a scan extract made of her file," the Angel told her. "You'll receive it in a few minutes."

The blue reception button on the ComWeb's telewriting attachment was glowing when Telzey came into her room. She closed the door, took the report tape on the Sirens from the reception slot, put the study reader she'd brought with her on a table, locked in the tape, and sat down. The report began flowing up over the reading screen at her normal scanning rate.

An exploration group had discovered the Sirens on a Terra-type world previously covered only sketchily by mapping teams. They were the planet's principal life-form, blanketing the landmasses in giant forests. The explorers soon discovered that a kind of euphoria, a pleasurable feeling of being drawn to them, was experienced by anyone coming within a few hundred yards of the pseudotrees. So they began referring to this life form as the Sirens.

It was a hospitable life-form. Every other creature found on the planet turned out to be a Siren parasite, living on the seemingly endless variety of edible items they produced. Tests disclosed surprisingly that many, perhaps all, of those items also satisfied human nutritional needs, and that most were pleasantly flavored. It wasn't long before half the expedition personnel were plucking their meals from the Sirens whenever they felt like it, in preference to resorting to their Hub supplies.

The notion of establishing this interesting and useful find in the Federation naturally arose. However, some caution seemed indicated in that there was reason to believe the Sirens had a potentially very high propagation rate, perhaps enough to make them a problem on civilized worlds. Two expedition ships presently carried Siren saplings and seedlings, along with other specimens from the planet, back to the Hub for further research.

At that time, several disconcerting discoveries were made almost simultaneously. A number of expedition members deserted together, leaving a message explaining that they intended to spend the rest of their lives among the Sirens, and it was realized belatedly that all who had been in contact with the Sirens for any length of time had developed varying degrees of emotional addiction to them. Then the ruins of a human colony, judged to be eight hundred years old, were unearthed; and the question of what had happened to the colonists on the Siren world was solved by the dissection of one of the parasitical specimens brought back to the Federation. Much of its internal structure still recognizably followed the human pattern. Without such evidence, no one could have suspected that this slow-moving, blind climber and crawler had branched away from the human species less than a thousand years ago.

It appeared that the Sirens induced other creatures to become dependent on them, and that even a highly evolved species then degenerated very rapidly to the point of becoming a true parasite, unable to survive away from its hosts. A space scan disclosed that two other worlds in that stellar area were also covered with Siren forests. On those worlds, too, there seemed to be no creatures left which hadn't become Siren parasites, and the indication was that their original human discoverers had introduced them to two associated colonies. In effect, all three human groups then had been wiped out. Their modified descendants could no longer be regarded as human in any significant sense.

The discovery of the Sirens wasn't publicized. General curiosity might be dangerous; there was a chance that Sirens could be transplanted to a civilization which wouldn't recognize their strange qualities until it was virtually destroyed. Various Overgovernment departments began making preparations for the sterilization of the three worlds. It seemed the only reasonable solution to the problem.

But there was somebody who wouldn't accept that.

The report didn't give the name of the former expedition member who argued that it wasn't the Sirens but their dangerous potential which should be eliminated, that they had intelligence, though it was intelligence so different from humanity's that it had been impossible for them to recognize the harm they did other creatures.

That couldn't be proved, of course. Not on the basis of what was generally known.

But neither could it be disproved—and the Overgovernment had been systematically alerted to the fact all along the line. A stop order went out on the preparation of sterilization measures. . . .

Telzey's lips quirked approvingly. Unless it could be shown that there was no alternative, or that a present emergency existed, the extermination or near-extermination of a species, let alone that of a species possessing sentient intelligence, was inexcusable under Federation law. The former expedition member had made a very good move. Investigations were now being conducted at various levels, though progress was hampered by the fact that investigators, unless given special protection, also became liable to Siren addiction.

"At present," the report concluded, "no sufficiently definite results appear to have been obtained."

The telewriting receiver had emitted a single bright *ping*-note a minute or two earlier, and the blue button was glowing again. Telzey dropped the tape on the Sirens into the room's disposal, and locked the tape on the determined former expedition member into the reader.

This extract was considerably shorter. Trigger Argee was twenty-six, had a high I.Q., had been trained in communications, administration, basic science, survival techniques, and unarmed combat at the Colonial School on Maccadon, had served in Precol on the world of Manon, and been employed in an administrative capacity on three U-League space expeditions. She was twice a pistol medalist, responsible, honest, had a good credit rating, and maintained a fashionable on-and-off marriage with an Intelligence Colonel. She'd been recently issued a temporary Class Four Clearance because of volunteer activities in connection with a classified Overgovernment project. Previous activities, not detailed in the extract, qualified her for a Class One Clearance if the need for it should arise.

The last was intriguing. Of the high-ranking people in the room below the balcony alcove, probably only Jessamine Amberdon held the Overgovernment's Class One Clearance. It might explain why Undersecretary Orsler and others had been unable to check the Siren crusade. Telzey dropped the extract into the disposal, made a mental note to check occasionally on the progress being made in the project.

When she got back down to the alcove, they were still talking in the room below, but it appeared that Orsler and his Guardian Angel had made their departure, the Angel presumably having provided Orsler with an unconscious motivation to leave. He believed in taking no chances with his charges.

Telzey grinned briefly, quietly gathered up her study materials and carried them back to her room.

2

The Regional Headquarters of the Psychology Service on Farnhart was housed in a tall structure of translucent green, towering in wilderness isolation above a northern ocean arm. Pilch stood in a gray Service uniform at a window of the office on the eightieth level which she'd taken over from the Regional Director that morning, gazing at the storm front moving in from the east. She was a slender woman, rather tall, with sable hair and ivory features, whose gray eyes had looked appraisingly on many worlds and their affairs.

"Trigger Argee," announced the communicator on the Director's desk behind her, "is on her way up here."

Pilch said, "Show her through to the office when she arrives." She went to the desk, placed a report file on it, turned to the side of the room where a large box stood on a table. Pilch touched one of the controls on the box. Its front wall became transparent. The lit interior contained what appeared to be a miniature tree planted in a layer of pebbly brown material. It stood about fifteen inches high, had a curving trunk and three short branches with a velvety appearance to them, and a dozen or so relatively large leaves among which nestled two white flower cups. It was an exquisitely designed thing, and someone not knowing better might have believed it to be a talented artist's creation. But it was alive; it was a Siren. Three months before, it had been a seedling. Left to itself, it would have stood three times Pilch's height by now. But its growth had been restrained, limiting it still to a seedling's proportions.

The office door dilated, and a mahogany-maned young woman in a green and gold business suit came in. She smiled at Pilch.

"Glad to see you!" she said. "I didn't know you were on Farnhart until I got your message."

Pilch said, "I arrived yesterday to handle some Service business. I'll leave again tonight. Meanwhile, here's your specimen, and copies of our investigators' reports."

"I'm sorry no one found anything positive," Trigger said. "I was beginning to feel we were on the right track finally."

"We won't assume it's the wrong track," said Pilch. "The results aren't encouraging, but what they amount to is that the xenotelepaths we had available weren't able to solve the problem. Various nonhuman xenos were called in to help and did no better. Neither, I'll admit, did I, when I was checking out the reports on the way here."

Trigger moistened her lips. "What *is* the problem?"

"Part of it," Pilch said, "is the fact that the investigations produced no indication of sentient intelligence. The Sirens' activities appear to be directed by complex instinctual drives.

And aside from that, your specimen is a powerhouse of psi. The euphoria it broadcasts is a minor manifestation, and we can assume that its ability to mutate other organisms is psi-based. But it remains an assumption. We haven't learned enough about it. Most of the xenos were unable to make out the psi patterns. They're very pronounced ones and highly charged, but oddly difficult to locate. Those who did recognize them and attempted to probe them experienced severe reactions. A few got into more serious trouble and had to be helped."

"What kind of trouble?" Trigger asked uneasily.

"Assorted mental disturbances. They've been straightened out again."

"Our little friend here did all that?"

"Why not? It may be as formidable as any adult Siren in that respect. The euphoric effect it produces certainly is as definite as that of the older specimens."

"Yes, that's true." Trigger looked at the box. "You're keeping a permanent psi block around it?"

"Yes. It can be turned off when contact is wanted."

Trigger was silent a moment, watching the Siren. She shook her head then. "I still don't believe they don't have intelligence!"

Pilch shrugged. "I won't say you're wrong. But if you're right, it doesn't necessarily improve the situation. The psi qualities that were tapped appear to be those of mechanism—a powerful mechanism normally inaccessible to alien psi contact. When contact is made, there is instant and violent reaction. If this is a reasoned response, the Siren seems to be an entity which regards any psi mind not of its own species as an enemy. There's no hesitation, no attempt to evaluate the contact."

"It may be a defensive reaction."

"True," Pilch said. "But it must be considered in conjunction with what else we know. The three Siren worlds appear sufficient evidence that the goal of the species is to take over all available space for itself. It has high mobility as a species, and evidently can cover any territory that becomes available to it with startling speed. As it spreads, all other life-forms present are converted to harmless parasites. This again, whether it's an instinctive process or a deliberate one, suggests the Siren is a being which tolerates only its own kind. Its apparent hospitality is a trap. It isn't a predator; it makes no detectable use of other forms of life. But it interrupts their evolutionary development and, in effect, eliminates them from the environment."

Trigger nodded slowly. "It's not a good picture."

"It's a damning picture," said Pilch. "Translated to human terms, this is, by every evaluation, a totally selfish, paranoid, treacherous, indiscriminately destructive species, a deadly danger to any other species it encounters. What real argument for its preservation can be made?"

Trigger gave her a brief smile.

"I'll argue that the picture is wrong!" she said. "Or, anyway, it's incomplete. If the Sirens, or their instincts, simply wanted to eliminate other creatures, there'd be no need for that very complicated process of turning them into parasites. One good chromosomal error for each new species they came across, and there'd be no next generation of that species around to annoy them!"

"Yes," Pilch said. "That's one reason, perhaps the only substantial reason so far, for not being too hasty about the Sirens." She paused. "Have you been getting any encouraging reports on the physical side of the investigation?"

Trigger shook her head. "Not recently. The fact is, the labs are licked—though some of them won't admit it yet."

"What we've learned about the specimen," said Pilch, "indicates they'll be forced to admit it eventually. If it weren't basically a psi problem, all the talent you've rounded up and put to work should have defanged the Sirens before this. The problem presumably will have to be solved on the psi level, if it's to be solved at all."

"It does seem so," Trigger agreed. She hesitated. "I'm trying to keep the labs plugging away a while longer mainly to gain time. If it's official that they've given up, the push to sterilize the Siren worlds will start again."

"It may be necessary to resort to that eventually," said Pilch. "They can't be left at large as they are. Even if the closest watch is maintained on those three worlds, something might go wrong."

"Yes, I know. It still would be a mistake, though," Trigger said. "Exterminating them might seem necessary because we hadn't been able to think of a good solution. But it would be a mistake, and wrong."

"You're convinced of it?"

"I am."

"Why?"

Trigger shook her head. "I don't know. Since I became un-addicted, I haven't even liked the Sirens much. It's not that I dislike them—I simply feel they're completely alien to me."

"How do you react now to the euphoria effect?" Pilch asked.

Trigger shrugged.

"It's an agreeable feeling. But I know it's an effect, and that makes it an agreeable feeling I'd sooner not have. It doesn't exactly bother me, but I certainly don't miss it when it's not there."

Pilch nodded. "There've been a few other occasions," she remarked, "when you've acted in a way that might have ap-peared dead wrong to any other rational human being. It turned out you were right."

"I know. You think I'm right about this?"

"I'm not saying that. But I feel your conviction is another reason for not coming to overly hurried conclusions about the Sirens." Pilch indicated the container. "What plans do you have for the specimen now?"

"I'm beginning to run a little short of plans," Trigger ad-mitted. "But I'll try the Old Galactics next. They're a kind of psi creature themselves, and they're good at working with liv-ing things. So I'll take the specimen to them."

Pilch considered. "Not a bad idea. They're still on Macca-don?"

"Very probably. They were there six months ago, the last time I visited Mantelish's garden. They weren't planning to move."

"When are you leaving?"

"Next ship out. Some time this afternoon."

Pilch nodded. "I'll be passing by Maccadon four days from now. I'll drop in then and contact you. And don't look so glum. We're not at the end of our rope. If it seems the Old Galactics can't handle the Sirens, I'll still have a few sugges-tions to make."

"Very glad to hear it!"

"And while we're on Maccadon," Pilch continued, "I'll have you equipped with a mind shield."

"A mind shield?" Trigger looked dubious. "I know they're

all using them in the labs, but . . . well, I had to wear one for a while last year. I didn't like it much."

"This will be a special design," Pilch told her. "It won't inconvenience you. If you're going to start escorting the specimen around again, you should have a good solid shield, just in case. We know that now."

3

In the rolling green highlands south of the city of Ceyce on Maccadon, Trigger's friend Professor Mantelish maintained a private botanical garden. It was his favorite retreat when he wanted to relax, though he didn't manage to get there often. Trigger herself would drop in now and then and stay for a week or two, sleeping in the room reserved for her use in the big white house which stood near the center of the garden.

The garden was where the Old Galactics lived. Only Trigger and Pilch knew they were there. Mantelish might have suspected it, though he'd never said so. Very few other people even knew of their existence. They'd had a great culture once, but it had been destroyed in a vast war which was fought and over with in the Milky Way before men learned how to dig mammoth pits. Not many Old Galactics survived that period, and they'd been widely scattered and out of contact, so that they had only recently begun to gather again. The garden appeared to be their reassembly area, and a whole little colony of them was there by now, arriving by mostly mysterious methods from various regions of the galaxy. That any at all of the fierce race which had attacked their culture still existed was improbable. The Old Galactics had formidable powers; and when they finally decided something needed to be eliminated, they were very thorough and patient about it.

Communication between them and humans was at best a laborious process. Trigger had done them a service some time before, and had learned how to conduct a conversation with Old Galactics on that occasion. They seemed to live on a different time scale. When you wanted to talk to them, you didn't try to hurry it.

So when she arrived at the garden with the Siren, she went first to her room in the house, steered the container on its gravity float to a table, settled it down on the tabletop and switched off the float. Then she unpacked, taking her time and putting everything away, arranging books she'd brought along on the shelves beside others she'd left here on her last visit. Afterward, Mantelish's housekeeper brought a lunch to the room, and Trigger ate that slowly and thoughtfully. Finally she selected a book and sat down with it.

All this time, she'd been letting the Old Galactic with whom she was best acquainted know she was here, and that she had a problem. She didn't push it, but simply brought the idea up now and then and let it, so to speak, drift around for a moment. Shortly after she'd settled down with the book, she got an acknowledgment.

The form it took was the image of one of the big trees in the garden, which came floating up in her mind. It wasn't the tree the Old Galactic had been occupying when she was here last, but they changed quarters now and then. She sent him a greeting, slipped the book into her jacket pocket, and left the room, towing the Siren container behind her.

By then, it was well into the spring afternoon. Three Tainequa gardeners were working near the great tree as she approached, small brown-skinned men, members of a little clan Mantelish had coaxed into leaving its terraced valley on Tainequa and settling on Maccadon to look after his collection. Trigger smiled and said hello to them; and they smiled back and then stood watching thoughtfully as she went on toward the tree, selected a place where she could sit comfortably among its roots, grounded the container, and took the book from her pocket.

When she looked up, the three Tainequas were walking quietly off along the path she'd come, carrying their tools, and in a moment they'd disappeared behind some shrubbery. Trigger wasn't surprised. The Tainequa valley people were marvelously skilled and versatile gardeners—entirely too good at their craft, in fact, not to understand very well that Mantelish's botanical specimens flourished to an extent even their talented efforts didn't begin to explain. And while they knew nothing about Old Galactics, they did believe in spirts, good and evil.

If they'd thought the local spirits were evil, the outrageous salary Mantelish was obliged to pay the clan couldn't have kept it on Maccadon another hour. Benevolent spirits, however, are also best treated with respect by mortal man. The Tainequas worked diligently elsewhere in the garden, but they kept their distance from the great trees which obviously needed no care from them anyway. And when Trigger sat familiarly down beside one, any Tainequa in sight went elsewhere. She wasn't quite sure what they thought her relationship with the spirits was, but she knew they were in some awe of her.

Under the circumstances, that was convenient. She didn't want anyone around to distract her. Actually, the Old Galactics did almost all the real work of carrying on the conversation, but she made it easier by remaining simultaneously relaxed and attentive and not letting her thoughts stray. So while she was looking down at the book on her knees, she wasn't reading. Her eyes, unfocused, blinked occasionally at nothing. She'd been invited to come; she'd come, and was waiting.

She waited, without impatience. Until presently:

Describe the problem.

She didn't sense it as words but as meaning, and sensed at the same time that there was more than one of them nearby, her old acquaintance among them. They liked the great trees of the garden as dwellings, their substance dispersed through the substance of the tree, flowing slowly through it like sap. They had their own natural solid shape when they chose to have it. And sometimes they took on other shapes for various purposes. Now a number of them had gathered near the base of the tree, still out of sight within it, to hear what she wanted.

She began thinking about the Sirens. The small one here in its container, and its giant relatives, mysterious and beautiful organisms, spread about three worlds in towering forests. She thought of how humans had encountered the Sirens and discovered how dangerous they were to other life, so dangerous that their complete extermination was beginning to look like the only logical way of dealing with them, and of her feeling that this would be totally wrong even if it seemed in the end to be inevitable. She didn't try to organize her thinking too much; what would get through to the Old Galactics were general impressions. They'd form their own concepts from that.

What do you want done?

She thought of the possibility that the Sirens had intelligence, and of reaching that intelligence and coming to an understanding with them so they would stop being uselessly destructive. Or, if they were creatures capable only of acting out of instinct, then ways might be found to modify them until they were no longer dangerous. The Old Galactics were great scientists in their own manner, which wasn't too similar to the human manner. Perhaps, Trigger's thoughts suggested, they would be able to succeed with the Sirens where humans so far had failed. She thought about the difficulties Pilch's xenotelepaths had encountered in trying to contact her specimen on the mental level, and of the fact that most humans had to be protected by psi blocks or mind shields against Siren euphoria.

There was stillness for a while then. She knew she'd presented the matter sufficiently, so she simply waited again. About an hour and a half had passed since she first sat down under the tree, which meant that from the Old Galactics' point of view they'd been having a very brisk conversational exchange.

By and by, something was told her.

Trigger nodded. "All right," she said aloud. She switched on the container's gravity float, moved it so that it stood next to the base of the big tree, and there grounded it again. Then she shut off the psi block, turned the front side transparent, opened the top, and sat down on a root nearby from where she could watch the Siren.

The euphoric effect became noticeable in a few seconds, strengthened gradually, then remained at the same level. It was always pleasurable, though everybody seemed to experience it in an individual manner. For Trigger it usually had been a light, agreeable feeling, which seemed a perfectly natural way to feel when she had it—a sense of well-being and contentment, an awareness that it came from being around Sirens, and a corresponding feeling of liking for them. In the course of time, that had been quite enough to produce emotional addiction in her; and other people had been much more directly and strongly affected. "That's it," she said now, for the Old Galactics' benefit.

There was no response from them; and time passed again, perhaps fifteen or twenty minutes. Then something began to emerge from the bark of the big tree above the container.

Trigger watched it. In its solid form, an Old Galactic looked something like a discolored sausage; and this was what now appeared to be moving out from the interior of the tree. It was a very slow process. It took a minute or two before Trigger could make out that this wasn't her acquaintance, who was sizable for his kind, but a much smaller Old Galactic, probably not weighing more than half a pound. It got clear of the tree at last, moved down a few inches until it was level with the top of the container, curved over to it, and started gliding down inside. Eventually then the sausage shape reached the base of the Siren, touched it, began melting into it.

Something else was said to Trigger. She hesitated questioningly a moment, then placed her wrist against the side of the root on which she was sitting and left it there. A minute or two afterward, a coolness touched the inside of her wrist. She couldn't see what caused it, but she knew. She also knew from experience that it harmed a human body no more than it harmed a tree to have an Old Galactic's substance dispersed through it; they were unnoticeable, and if there was anything wrong with the body when they entered, they would take care of it before they left, precisely as they tended to the botanical specimens in Mantelish's garden.

In this case, they weren't concerned about Trigger's health, which was excellent. But they evidently felt, as had Pilch, that if she was going to be involved with a Siren, she should have the protection of a mind shield; and an Old Galactic specialist was now to begin providing her with their equivalent of one. He should be finished with the job in a few days. Trigger asked some questions about it, was given explanations, and presently agreed then to let the specialist go ahead.

The rest of the afternoon passed uneventfully, as far as she was concerned. They'd told her after a while to restore the psi block and close the container. She was glad to do it. It was unlikely that a Tainequa would approach this section of the garden again today and get within range of the euphoria effect, but one never knew just what might happen if an area was exposed to the effect for any extended period of time. After that, the Old Galactics ignored her. She read in her book a while, stretched out in the grass near the tree for a nap, read some more. Eventually it was getting near evening, and there still had been no indication that the Old Galactics intended to interrupt whatever they were doing. Trigger went to the garden house, came back with her supper, a sleeping bag, and a few more books. She ate, read until dark, then opened the bag, got into it, and fell asleep.

She dreamed presently that she was back in a great Siren forest on a faraway world, swimming in the euphoria experience, but now frightened by it because she was aware she was becoming addicted. She made a violent effort to escape, and the effort brought her awake.

She knew where she was immediately then. A cloud bank covered the sky, with the starblaze gleaming through here and there; the garden lay quiet and shadowy around her. But the sense of Siren euphoria hadn't faded with the dream.

Trigger turned over, slipped partly out of the sleeping bag, and sat up. She couldn't make out the Siren container too well in the shade of the great tree, but she could see that it had been opened; and the psi block obviously was switched off. She had a moment of alarm. Then Old Galactic thought brushed slowly past her.

They weren't addressing her, and she couldn't make out any meaning. But she saw now that several dark sausage shapes of varying sizes were on the container. A vague thought pulse touched her mind again. It was ridiculous to think of Old Galactics becoming excited about anything; but Trigger had the impression that the little group on the container was as close to excitement as it could get. One of them evidently touched the psi block control then because the euphoria effect went out.

She sat there a while longer watching them and wondering what they were doing; but nothing much happened and she had no more thought impressions. Presently they began to move back to the big tree and into it. The last one shifted the control that closed the container before turning to follow his companions. Trigger got down into the bag again and went back to sleep. When she woke up next, it was cool dawn in the garden, everything looking pale and hazy. And the Old Galactics were speaking to her.

She gathered that the matter looked quite favorable, but

that they couldn't give her definite information yet. One of them was still inside the Siren, analyzing it. She was to take the container back to her room now, and return with it in the evening. Then they would be able to tell her more.

4

"Well?" Pilch inquired, when they met two days later in Ceyce.

"They can do it," Trigger said. "They couldn't explain how—at least not in a way I understood."

"You hardly look overjoyed," Pilch observed. "What's the hitch?"

Trigger shrugged. "The time element. They live so long, they never really seem to understand how important time is to us. Getting the Sirens tamed down would take them a while."

"How much of a while?"

"That was a little blurry. Anything having to do with time tends to be with them. But I'm afraid they meant something like a couple of centuries."

Pilch shook her head. "We can't wait that long!"

"I know," Trigger said. "What I told them was that I was in a little bit of a hurry with the Sirens, so I'd better shop around for faster results."

"How did they react?"

"They seemed to think it was a good idea. So—I'm on the move again." Trigger smiled soberly. "What are the other approaches you had in mind?"

"At the moment, I have two suggestions," said Pilch. "There are a few Service xenos in whom I'd have some confidence in the matter. They're among our best operators. However, they're on an assignment outside the Hub. Even if they were to interrupt what they're doing—which they shouldn't—it would take them well over a month to get here."

"I'll be glad to take the specimen to them," said Trigger.

Pilch nodded. "We may wind up having you do just that. On the other hand, you may need to go no farther than

Orado. There's a psi there who's a very capable xenotelepath. She isn't in the Service and doesn't let it be generally known that she's a psi. But if she feels like it, it's quite possible she'll be able to determine whether the Sirens have intelligence, and whether it's a type and degree of intelligence that will permit communication with them. If that should turn out to be the case, of course, we'd be over the first great hurdle."

"We certainly would be!" Trigger agreed. "How do I get in touch with her?"

Pilch produced a card. "Here's her name and current address. Send her a teleletter, outline the situation, inquire whether she'd like to investigate the specimen for you, and so forth. If she'll do it, she's your best present bet."

"I'll get at it immediately." Trigger studied the card, put it in her purse. "Telzey Amberdon. How much can I tell her?"

"Anything you like. Telzey's come by more information about the Federation's business than most members of the Council should have. But she doesn't spill secrets. I'll give you a Class Four Clearance to send her, to keep it legitimate."

"What kind of fee will she want?" asked Trigger. "I might have to make arrangements."

"I doubt she'll want a fee. Her family has plenty of money. She'll work for you if the proposition catches her interest. Otherwise, she won't."

"I should be able to make it sound interesting enough," Trigger remarked. "Supposing she gets herself into trouble over this like some of your xenos?"

Pilch said, "Nobody's suffered permanent damage so far. If she winds up needing therapeutic help, she'll get it. I wouldn't worry too much. Telzey's a little monster in some respects. But I'll be around the area a while, and you can contact me through any Service center." She looked at her timepiece. "We'll go to the Ceyce lab now, and get you equipped with your mind shield."

"Well, as to *that*," said Trigger, "I already have one. Not quite, but very nearly."

"Eh?"

Trigger explained about her resident Old-Galactic, and that he'd been doing something to her nervous system for the past two days. They went to the Service lab anyway; Pilch wanted to know just what was being done to Trigger's nervous system. Tests established then that she, indeed, had a shield. It permitted contact with her conscious thoughts but sealed off the rest of her mind with a block which stopped the heaviest probe Pilch tried against it. However, it was a block which became nonexistent when Trigger didn't want it there.

"Any time I decide to get rid of it permanently, it will start fading away," Trigger said.

Pilch nodded. "I noticed there'd been provision made for that." She reflected. "Well, you won't need the shield I'd intended for you. They're giving you something that seems more effective. So I'll be running along."

She left. Around evening of that day, Trigger's Old Galactic let her know he'd finished his work. She went back to his home tree and held her wrist against it until he'd transferred again, thanked them all around for their trouble, and returned to her room. The letter to Telzey Amberdon was already prepared. It didn't mention the Old Galactics but was candid about almost everything else, specifically the subject of risks. Trigger flew in to Ceyce and had the letter dispatched to Orado at an interstellar transmitter station. Telzey Amberdon should receive it some six hours later.

That night, after the lights were out in the garden house and Trigger was asleep in her room, a visitor came to Mantelish's garden. Three Tainequas on their way to their quarters saw, but didn't notice, the cloaked shape moving toward them under the starblaze, went on talking in their soft voices, unaware of the shadow drifting across their minds, unaware of the visitor passing them a few feet away.

Pilch moved deeper into the garden and into the dimness under the great trees. Now and then she stopped and stood quietly, head turning this way and that, like a sensing animal, and went on in a new direction. At last, she halted before the tree where Trigger had conferred with the Old Galactics, and stayed there.

Awareness stirred in the tree, slowly focused on her. There was a long pause. An inquiry came.

Pilch identified herself. After a time, the identification was acknowledged. *Your purpose?*

She brought up assorted unhurried impressions of Trigger's Siren specimen, of the Siren worlds, of the effects produced by Sirens, of their inaccessibility to psi contact. . . .

Yes. The Hana species.

What did they know if it?

Pilch gathered presently that they'd never encountered a Hana before this. They'd had reports. Not recent ones. They'd believed the species was extinct.

Was it as dangerous as it appeared to be?

Yes. Very dangerous.

The slow exchange continued. In Pilch's mind, impressions formed. Time, space, and direction remained wavering, unstable concepts. But, by any human reckoning, it must have been very long ago, very far away in the galaxy's vastness, that a race of conquerors brought Hanas to many civilized worlds. Presently those worlds were destroyed. The Hanas had swifter weapons than their ability to produce euphoria and mindless dependency in other species. Pilch watched as psi death lanced out from them, and all other minds in a wide radius winked out of existence. She saw great psi machines brought up to control the Hanas, and then those machines shredded into uselessness as their own energies stormed wildly through them. On a planet, while a semblance of its surface remained, the Hana species seemed indestructible, spreading and proliferating like a shifting green flood, sweeping up into furious life here as it was annihilated there.

They died at last when distant space weapons seared all worlds, many hundreds of worlds by then, on which they were to be found until no life of any kind remained possible. Then the great race the Hana had fought hunted long and far, to make sure none remained alive in the universe.

But it appeared that one remote planet, at least, had been overlooked in that search.

Near daybreak, a small aircar lifted from a forested hillside a little to the north of Mantelish's garden and sped away toward Ceyce. Trigger awoke an hour later, had breakfast, watched a few Tainequas moving about the garden from the veranda of her room, settled down to read. Around noon, the telewriter in Mantelish's office on the ground floor began clanging. Trigger hurried down, took a letter capsule from the receiver.

It appeared Telzey Amberdon's time next week would be mainly occupied with college graduation exams. However, she did want to see Miss Argee's Siren and discuss her plan with her, and would be pleased to meet her on Orado. If it happened to be convenient to Miss Argee, she had the coming weekend free—that being Days Seventy-one and Seventy-two of the standard year.

It was now Day Seventy. Trigger called the Psychology Service Center in Ceyce and left a message for Pilch. She packed quickly, loaded the Siren container into her aircar, and headed for Ceyce Port. Within the hour, she was on her way to Orado.

5

Trigger met Telzey Amberdon next morning in a room she'd taken in the Haplandia Hotel at the Orado City Space Terminal. She was startled for a moment by the fact that Telzey seemed to be at most seventeen years old. On reflection, she decided then that a capable young psi, one who knew more Federation secrets than most Council members, might mature rather rapidly.

"Ready to be euphorized?" she asked, by and by.

Telzey nodded. "Let's check it out."

Trigger switched off the psi block on the Siren container, and Siren euphoria began building up gradually in the room. Telzey leaned forward in her chair, watching the Siren. Her expression grew absent as if she were listening to distant voices. Trigger, having seen a similar expression on Pilch now and then, remained silent. After a minute or two, Telzey straightened, looked over at her.

"You can shield it again," she said.

Trigger restored the psi block. "What was it like?"

"Very odd! There was a wisp of psi sense for a moment— just as you switched off the block."

Trigger looked interested and thoughtful. "No one else reported that."

"It was there. But it was gone at once, and I didn't get it again. The rest was nothing. Almost like a negation of psi! I felt as if I were reaching into a vacuum."

Trigger nodded. "That's more or less how the Service xenos

describe the sensation. I brought along a file of their reports. Like to see them?"

Telzey said she would. Trigger produced the file; and Telzey sat down at a table with it and began scanning through the reports. Trigger watched her. A likable sort of young person . . . strong-willed probably. Intelligent certainly. Capable of succeeding where Pilch's xenos had failed? Trigger wondered. Still, Pilch wouldn't have referred to her as a little monster without reason.

The little monster presently closed the file and glanced over at Trigger.

"That certainly *is* a different kind of psi creature!" she remarked. "Different from anything I've come across, anyway. I don't know if I can do anything with it. I'm not your last hope, am I?"

Trigger smiled briefly. "Not the last. But the next one's more than a month's travel time away."

"Do you want me to try? Now that you've seen me?"

Trigger hesitated. "It's not exactly a matter of wanting anyone to try."

"You're worried, aren't you?" Telzey asked.

"Yes, I'm worried," Trigger acknowledged. "I seem to be getting a little more worried all the time."

"What about?"

Trigger bit her lip gently. "I can't say specifically. It may be my imagination. But I don't think so. It's a feeling that we'd better get this business with the Sirens straightened out."

"Or something might happen?"

"That's about it. And that the situation might be getting more critical the longer it remains unsettled."

Telzey studied her quizzically. "Then why aren't you anxious to have me try the probe?"

Trigger said, "There hasn't been too much trouble so far. In the labs, where they've been trying to modify the Sirens biologically, there's been no trouble at all. Except, of course, that some people got addiction symptoms before they started using psi blocks and mind shields. But you see, all they've accomplished in the labs is to put some checks on the Sirens." She indicated the container. "Like stopping this one's growth, keeping the proliferation cycles from getting started, and so on. Meanwhile, there've been indications that the chromosomal changes involved have gradually begun to reverse—which, I've been told by quite a number of people, is impossible."

Telzey said, "The midget here might start to grow again?"

"Yes, it might. What it means is that the labs haven't really got anywhere. Now, the Psychology Service xenos didn't get too far either, but they did learn a few definite things about the Siren. They got into trouble immediately."

Telzey nodded.

"And you," Trigger said, "are supposed to be better than the Service xenos. You should be able to go further. If you do, it's quite possible you'll get into more serious trouble than they did."

Telzey said after a moment, "You think the Siren doesn't intend to change from what it is? Or let us find out what it really is?"

"It almost looks that way, doesn't it?"

"On the psi side it might look that way," Telzey agreed. She smiled. "You know, you're not trying very hard to push me into this!"

"No," Trigger said. "I'm not trying to push you into it. I don't feel I should. I feel I should tell you what I think before you decide."

Telzey looked reflective. "You told other people?"

Trigger shook her head. "If I started talking about it generally, it might turn us back to the extermination program. I think that's the last thing that should happen." She added, "Pilch probably knows. She's looked around in my mind now and then, for one reason and another. But she hasn't said anything."

"Pilch is the one who recommended me to you?" Telzey asked.

"Yes. Have you met?"

Telzey shook her head. "I've never heard of her. What's she like?"

Trigger considered.

"Pilch is Pilch," she said. "She has her ways. She's a very good psi. She seems to be one of the Service's top executives. She's a busy lady, and I don't think she'd bother herself for a minute with the Sirens if she thought they weren't important. She told me there was a definite possibility you'd be able to get into communication with our specimen—that's assuming,

of course, there's something there that can communicate."
Trigger thought again, shrugged. "I've known Pilch nearly
two years, but that's almost all I can tell you about her."

Telzey was silent for over a minute now, dark-blue eyes
fixed reflectively on Trigger.

"If I told you," she said suddenly, "that I didn't want to get
involved in this, what would you do?"

"Get packed for a month's travel plus," Trigger said
promptly. "I don't think it will be at all safe to push ahead on
the psi side here, but I think it will be safer generally than not
pushing ahead."

Telzey nodded.

"Well, I am getting involved," she said. "So that's settled.
We'll see if Pilch is right, and it's something I can handle—
and whether you're right, and it's something that has to be
handled. I can't quite imagine the Sirens as a menace to the
Federation, but we'll try to find out more about them. If I
don't accomplish anything, you can still pack up for that
month's trip. How much time can you spend on Orado now?"

Trigger said, "As much time as it takes, or you're willing to
put in on it."

Telzey asked, "Where will you stay? We can't very well
work in the Haplandia."

"We certainly can't," Trigger agreed. "We'd have half the
hotel in euphoria if we left the Siren unshielded for ten minutes. I haven't made arrangements yet. The labs where they
work on Sirens are all a good distance away from population
centers, even though the structures are psi-blocked. So I'll be
looking for a place that's well out in the country, but still convenient for you."

"I know a place like that."

"Yes?"

"My family has a summer house up in the hills," Telzey
said. "Nobody will be using it the next couple of months.
There's Ezd Malion, the caretaker; but he and his wife have
their own house a quarter of a mile away."

Trigger nodded. "They'll be safe there. Unless there are
special developments. The Siren euphoria couldn't do more
than give them sunny dispositions at that distance."

"That's what I thought from the reports," said Telzey.
"And we can keep the Malions away from the house while
we're working. There's nobody else around for miles. It's con-

venient for me—I can get there from college in twenty minutes. . . . If there isn't something you want to do, why don't
we move you and the Siren in this afternoon?"

6

The Hana dwarf dreamed in its own way occasionally. Its
life of the moment had been a short one and might not be extended significantly; but its ancestral memory went back for a
number of generations before it began to fade, and beyond
that was a kind of memory to which it came only when it
withdrew its attention wholly from the life of the moment and
its requirements. It had taken to doing it frequently since realizing it was on a Veen world and no longer in contact with its
kind.

That form of memory went back a long way to the world
on which the Hanas originated, and even to the early period
of that world when they gained supremacy after dangerous
and protracted struggles with savage species as formidable as
they. They came at last to the long time in which the world
remained in harmony and they kept it so, living the placid and
thoughtful plant existence they preferred, but not unaware of
what went on outside. Disruptions occurred occasionally
when some form of scurrying mobile life, nervously active,
eternally eating or being eaten, began to become a nuisance,
to crowd out others, or attempt to molest the Hanas. Then the
Hanas would beckon that overly excitable species to them and
start it on the path which led it eventually to the quietly satisfactory existence of the plant.

It was a good time, and the Hana dwarf now lived there
often for a while before returning, strenghtened, to the life of
the moment and the knowledge of being among the Veen.
There was little else to do. The Veen held it enclosed in a cage
of energy, difficult to penetrate and opened only when they
came with their prying minds and mind machines to seek out
and enslave the captured Hana mind, precisely as they had
done in other days. They'd learned much in the interval, if not

greater wisdom and less arrogance. The Hana dwarf was aware of the manipulations which stopped its growth and prevented it from developing and distributing its seed. But such things were of no significance. They could be undone. The question was whether the Veen could reach its mind.

It hadn't believed they could. It was more formidably armed than any Hana had been in the times of the Veen War; if its defenses failed, the touch of its thought would kill other minds in moments. But it was less sure now. The Veen's first probes barely reached its defenses, broke there; and a brief period of quiet followed. But they were persistent. Indications came that another attempt was being carefully prepared, with mind qualities involved which had not been noticeable before.

It would warn them, though Veen had not yet been known to respond sensibly to a warning. They were the race which knew no equals, which could tolerate only slaves. If they persisted and succeeded, the Hana would emerge to kill, and presently to die. A single pulse would be enough to notify the Three Worlds, long since alerted, and waiting now with a massed power never before encountered by Veen, that the Veen War had been resumed.

The Hana shaped its warnings and set them aside, to be released as seemed required. Then, with its several deaths prepared, it, too, waited, and sometimes dreamed.

Toward evening, four days after Trigger and the Siren specimen moved into the Amberdon summer house, Telzey was on her way there by aircar. It had been a demanding day at college, but she was doing very well in the exams. When she left Pehanron, she'd felt comfortabley relaxed.

Some five minutes ago then, her mood shifted abruptly. An uneasy alertness awoke in her. It wasn't the first time she'd felt that way during the past few days.

The Siren? From behind a psi block and over all these miles? Not likely but perhaps not impossible either. She hadn't made much headway in the investigation over the weekend and the last two evenings, and hadn't tried to. That was a strange being! Under the mechanical euphoric effect seemed to lie only the empty negation which had met her first probe. The Service's translating machines had reported nothing at all, but most of the Service xenotelepaths also had sensed the void, the emptiness, the vacuum. Some of them eventually found something in the vacuum. They weren't sure of what they'd found; but they'd stirred up a violence and power difficult to associate with the midget Siren. Mind shields had been hard tested. Some shields weren't tight enough or resistant enough; and as a result, the Service had a few lunatic xenos around for a while.

Even without Trigger's forebodings, it wouldn't have looked like a matter to rush into. When the exams were over, Telzey could settle down to serious work on the Siren. All she'd intended during the week was to become acquainted with it.

In doing even that much, had she allowed it to become acquainted with her? She wasn't sure. Something or other, at any rate, seemed to have developed an awareness of her. Otherwise, she'd had no problems. The addictive effect didn't bother her; that could be dampened or screened out, and whatever lingered after a period of contact was wiped from her mind in seconds.

The something-or-other did bother her.

Telzey turned the aircar into the mouth of a wide valley. It was between winter and spring in the hills, windy and wet. Snow still lay in the gullies and along the mountain slopes, but the green things were coming awake everywhere. The Amberdon house stood forty miles to the north above the banks of a little lake. . . .

There was this restlessness, a frequent inclination to check the car's view screens, though there was almost no air traffic here. Simply a feeling of something around! Something unseen.

When it happened before, she'd suspected there might be a psi prowling in her mental neighborhood, somebody who was taking an interest in her. Since such uninvited interest wasn't always healthy, she'd long since established automatic sensors which picked up the beginnings of a scanning probe and simultaneously concealed and alerted her. The sensors hadn't gone into action.

So it shouldn't be a human psi hanging around. Unless it was a psi with a good deal defter touch than she'd encountered previously. Under the circumstances, that, too, wasn't impossible.

If it wasn't a human psi, it almost had to be a Siren manifestation.

The feeling faded before she reached the house and brought her Cloudsplitter down to the carport. Another aircar stood there, the one Trigger had rented for her stay on Orado.

During the past two evenings, they'd established a routine. When Telzey arrived from college, she and Trigger had dinner, then settled down in the room Gilas Amberdon used as a study when he was in the house. Its main attraction was a fine fireplace. They'd talk about this and that; meanwhile the Siren's unshielded container stood on a table in a corner of the room, and Telzey's thoughts drifted about the alien strangeness, not probing in any way but picking up whatever was to be learned easily. She soon stopped getting anything new in that manner; what was to be learned easily about the Siren remained limited. Some time before midnight, they'd restore the psi block, and Telzey went off to Pehanron.

But before she left, they turned on the lights in the grounds outside for a while. The very first night, the day Trigger and the Siren moved in, they'd had a rather startling experience. They were in the study when they began to hear sounds outside. It might have been tree branches beating against the wall in the wind, except that no tree grew so close to the house there. It might even have been an unseasonal, irregular spattering of hail. The study had no window, but the adjoining room had two, so they went in, opened a window and looked out.

At once, something came up over the sill with a great wet flap of wings and tail and drove into the room between them, bowling Telzey over. Trigger yelped and slammed the window shut as another pair of wings boomed in from the windy dusk with more shadowy shapes behind it. When she looked around, Telzey was getting to her feet and the intruder had disappeared into the house. They could hear it flapping about somewhere.

"Are you hurt, Telzey?"

"No."

"What in the world is that thing? There's a whole mess of them outside!"

"Eveers. They're on spring migration. A flock was probably settling to the lake and got in range of the Siren."

"Good Lord, yes! The Siren! We should have realized—what'll we do with the one in the house?"

"The first thing we'd better do is get the Siren shielded," said Telzey.

Trigger cocked her head, listening. "The, uh, eveer is in the study!"

Telzey laughed. "They're not very dangerous. Come on!"

The eveer might not have been a vicious creature normally, but it had strong objections to being evicted from the study and put up a determined fight. They both collected beak nips and scratches, were knocked about by solid wing strokes and thoroughly muddied by the eveer's wet hide, before they finally got it pinned down under a blanket. Then Trigger crouched on the blanket, panting, while Telzey restored the psi block. After that, the eveer seemed mainly interested in getting away from them. They carried it to the front door between them, bundled in the blanket, and opened the door. There they recoiled.

A sizable collection of Orado's local walking and flying fauna had gathered along the wall of the house. But the creatures were already beginning to disperse, now that the Siren's magic had faded; and at the appearance of the two humans, most of them took off quickly. Trigger and Telzey shook the eveer out of the blanket, and it went flapping away heavily into the night.

It took them most of an hour to tend to their injuries and clean up behind it. After that, they ignored unusual sounds outside the house when the container's psi block was off.

Other things were less easy to ignore.

The night Telzey started back to Pehanron after the weekend was the time she first got the impression that something unseen was riding along with her. Psi company, she suspected, though her sensors reported nothing. She waited a while, relaxed her mind screens gradually, sent a sudden quick, wide search-thought about, with something less friendly held in readiness, in case it was company she didn't like. The search-thought should have caught at least a trace of whoever or whatever was there. It didn't.

She remained behind her screens then, waiting. The feeling grew no stronger; sometimes it seemed to weaken. But it was a good five minutes before it faded completely.

It came back twice in the next two days. Once in the house while she was in the study with Trigger, once on the way to the house. She didn't mention it to Trigger; but that night, when it was getting time for her to leave, she said, "I think I'll sleep here tonight and start back early in the morning."

"Be my guest," Trigger said affably. She hesitated, added, "The fact is I'll be rather glad to know you're around."

Telzey looked at her. "You get lonesome at night in this big old house?"

"Not exactly lonesome," Trigger said. "I've never minded being by myself." She smiled. "Has your house ever had the reputation of being haunted?"

"Haunted? Not for around a hundred years. You've had the impression there's a spook flitting about?"

"Just an odd feeling occasionally," Trigger said. She paused, added in a changed voice, "And by coincidence, I'm beginning to get that feeling again now!"

They stood silent then, looking at each other. The feeling grew. It swelled into a sensation of bone-chilling cold, of oppressive dread. It seemed to circle slowly about them, drawing closer. Telzey passed her tongue over her lips. Psi slashed out twice. The sensation blurred, was gone.

She turned toward the Siren container. Trigger shook her head. "The psi block's on," she said. "It was on the other times, too. I checked."

And the psi block was on. Telzey asked, "How often has it happened?"

Trigger shrugged. "Four or five times. I'll come awake at night. It'll last a minute or two and go away."

"Why didn't you tell me?"

"I didn't want to disturb you," Trigger said. "It wasn't as strong as this before. I didn't know what it was, but it didn't seem to have anything to do with the Siren." She smiled, a trifle shakily. "An Amberdon ghost I could stand."

"Let's sit down," Telzey said. "It wasn't an Amberdon ghost, but it was a ghost of sorts."

They sat down. "What do you mean?" Trigger asked.

Telzey said, "A psi structure. Something with some independent duration. A fear ghost. A psi mind made it, planted it. It was due to be sensed when we sensed it."

Trigger glanced at the container. "The Siren?"

"Yes, the little Siren." Telzey blinked absently, fingering her chin. "There was nothing human about that structure. So the Siren put it out while the block was off. It's telling us not to fool around with it. . . . But now we *will* have to fool around with it!"

Trigger looked questioningly at her.

"It means you were right," Telzey said. "The Siren has intelligence. It knows there's somebody around who's trying to probe it, and it doesn't want to be probed. It's tried to use fear to drive us away. Any psi mind that can put out a structure like that is very good! Dangerously good." She shook her head. "I don't think anyone could say exactly what a whole world of creatures who can do that mightn't be able to do otherwise!"

"Three worlds," said Trigger.

"Yes, three worlds. So the Siren operation can't just stop. They don't know enough about us. They might think we're very dangerous to them, and, of course, we are dangerous. The three worlds are there, and sooner or later somebody's going to do something stupid about them. And something will get started—if it hasn't started already." She glanced at Trigger, smiled briefly. "Until now, I was thinking it might be only your imagination! But it isn't. This is a really bad matter."

Trigger said after a moment, "I wish it had been only my imagination!" She looked at the Siren container. "You still think you can handle it?"

Telzey shrugged. "I wouldn't know by myself. But I'm sure Pilch gave that careful consideration."

Trigger reflected, tongue tip between lips, nodded. "Yes, she must have. It seems you've been pushed into something, Telzey."

"We've both been pushed into something," Telzey said.

Trigger sighed. "Well, I can't blame her too much! It has to be done, and the Service couldn't do it—at least not quickly enough. But I won't blame you at all if you want to pull out."

"I might want to pull out," Telzey admitted. "It's more than I'd counted on. But I'd be going around worrying about the Sirens then, like you've been doing. We know more now to be worried about."

"So you're staying?"

"Yes."

Trigger smiled. "I can't say I'm sorry! Look. It's getting late, and you'll have to be off to college early. Let's talk about strictly noneerie things for a little, and turn in."

So they talked about noneerie matters, and soon went to bed, and slept undisturbed until morning, when Telzey flew off to Pehanron College.

That evening, she slipped a probe lightly into the psi-emptiness of the Siren—an area she'd kept away from since her first contact with it. She thought presently it didn't seem quite as empty as it had. There might be something there. Something perhaps like a vague, distant shadow, only occasionally and briefly discernible.

She withdrew the probe carefully.

"Let's leave the psi block on until I've finished with the exams," she told Trigger later. "I've picked up as much as I can use for a start." She wasn't so sure now of the psi block's absolute dependability when it came to the Siren. But it should act as a temporary restraint.

Trigger didn't comment. Telzey slept in the house the rest of the week, and nothing of much significance happened. What remained of the exams wasn't too significant either; she went breezing through it all with only half her attention. Then the end of the week came, and she moved into the summer house. In three weeks, she'd be attending graduation ceremonies at Pehanron College. Until then, her time was her own.

7

It was early on the first morning after the exams then that Telzey had her first serious session with the Siren. She'd closed the door to the study and moved an armchair to a point from where she could observe the container. Trigger wasn't present; she'd stay out in the house to avoid distracting Telzey, and to handle interruptions like ComWeb calls. Ezd Malion, the caretaker, usually checked in before noon to get shopping instructions.

Telzey settled herself in the chair, relaxed physically. Mentally there'd be no relaxing. If the Siren entity followed the reaction pattern described in the Service reports, she shouldn't be running into immediate problems. But it might not stay with the pattern.

Her probe moved cautiously into the psi-emptiness. After a time, she gained again the impression of a few days before: it wasn't as empty as it had appeared at first contact. Something shadowy, distant, seemed to be there.

She began to work with the impression. What did she feel about it? A vague thing—and large. Cold perhaps. Yes. Cold and dark. . . .

It was what she felt, no more than that. But her feelings were all she had to work with at this stage. Out of them other things could develop. There was this vague, dark, cold large-ness then, connected with the Siren on the study table. She tried to gain some impression of the relationship.

An impression came suddenly, a negative one. The relation-ship had been denied. Afterward, the darkness seemed to have become a little colder. Telzey's nerves tingled. There was no change otherwise, but she'd had a response. Her psi sensors reached toward the fringes of the darkness, seemed to touch it, still found nothing that allowed a probe. She had a symbol of what was there, not yet its reality. But the search had moved on a step.

Then there was an interruption. She knew suddenly she wasn't alone in the study. This was much more definite than any previous feeling that there might be someone or some-thing about. She still sensed nothing specific, but the hair at the nape of her neck was trying to lift, and the skin of her back prickled with awareness of another's presence in the room.

Telzey didn't look around, knowing she'd see no one if she did. Instead, she flicked a search probe out suddenly. As sud-denly the presence was gone.

She sat quiet a moment, returned her attention to the sym-bol. Nothing there had changed. She withdrew from it, stood up, turned the container's psi block back on, and looked at her watch. About an hour had passed since she'd entered the study.

She found Trigger in the conservatory, tending to the plants under the indoor sun. "Trigger," she said, "did you happen to be thinking about me a few minutes ago?"

"Probably," Trigger said. "I've been thinking about you right along, wondering how you were doing. Why?"

"Has there ever been anything to indicate you might be a psi?"

Trigger looked surprised.

"Well," she said, "I understand everybody's a bit of a psi. So I suppose I'm that. I've never done anything out of the ordinary, though. Except perhaps—" She hesitated.

"Except perhaps what?" Telzey asked.

Trigger told her about the Old Galactics and her contacts with them.

"Great day in the morning!" Telzey said, astounded, when Trigger concluded. "You certainly have unusual acquaintances!"

"Of course, no one's to know they're there," Trigger remarked.

"Well, I won't tell."

"I know you won't. You think it might mean I'm a kind of telepath?"

"It might," Telzey said. "It wouldn't have to. They may simply have themselves tuned in on you." She stood a moment, reflecting. "I ran into a heavy-duty psi once who didn't have the faintest idea he was one," she said. "It was a problem because all sorts of extraordinary things kept happening to him and around him. Right now, anything like that could be disturbing."

Trigger looked concerned. "Have there been disturbances?"

"I haven't noticed anything definite," Telzey said untruthfully. "But I've been wondering."

"Could you find out about me if I undid that mind shield they gave me?"

Telzey sat down. "Let's try."

Trigger wished the shield out of existence. Some little time passed. Then Telzey said, "You can put the shield back."

"Well?" Trigger asked. "Am I?"

"You are," Telzey said absently. "I thought you might be, from the way you've been worrying about the Sirens." She shook her head. "Trigger, that's the most disorganized psi mind I've ever contacted! I wonder why Pilch never mentioned it."

Trigger hesitated. "Now that *you've* mentioned it," she said, "I believe Pilch did suggest something of the kind on one occasion. I thought I'd misunderstood her. She didn't refer to it again."

"Well, if you like," said Telzey, "we can take a week off after we're through with the Siren, and see if we can't make you operational."

Trigger rubbed her nose tip. "Frankly, I doubt that I'd want to be operational."

"Why?"

"You and Pilch seem to thrive on it," Trigger said, "but I've met other psis who weren't cheery people. I suppose you can pick up a whole new parcel of problems when you have abilities like that."

"You pick up problems, all right," Telzey acknowledged.

"That's what I thought, And I," Trigger said, "seem to find all the problems I can handle without adding complications. Could that disorganized psi mind of mine do anything to disturb you when you're trying to work with the Siren?"

Telzey shook her head. Trigger, psi-latent, hadn't been unconsciously responsible for those manifestations, couldn't have been. Neither was the Siren. This time, there'd been, for a moment, a decidedly human quality about the immaterial presence.

So the Psychology Service was keeping an eye on proceedings here. She'd half expected it. And they'd assigned an operator of exceptional quality to the job—*she* couldn't have prowled about an alerted telepath and remained as well concealed.

Nor, Telzey thought, was that the only concealed high-quality psi around. While Trigger was talking about the Old Galactics, she'd recalled that flick of mind-stuff she caught the moment the Siren container came unshielded in the Haplandia Hotel.

It seemed the Old Galactics, too, had an interest in the Siren specimen, and were represented in the summer house. . . .

Did either of them know about the other? Did the Siren entity know about either of them, or suspect it had an occupant? It was nothing she could mention to Trigger—there was too much psi involved all around, and Trigger's surface thoughts were accessible to any telepath who wanted to follow them.

She'd have to await developments—and meanwhile push ahead toward the probe. Around that point, everything should start falling into place. It would have to.

She told Trigger what she'd accomplished so far, added, "I've probably got the contact process started. This afternoon

I'll pick the symbol up again and see." She yawned, stretched slowly. "How about we go for a long walk before lunch? This is great hiking country."

They went down to the end of the grounds, past the house where Ezd Malion and his wife lived, and on to the banks of the lake. The sun was out that morning; it was chilly, blustery, refreshing. They followed narrow trails used more often by animals than by people. It was over an hour before they turned back for lunch.

Early in the afternoon then, Telzey went into the study and closed the door. She emerged four hours later. Trigger regarded her with some concern. "You look pretty worn out!"

"I am pretty worn out," Telzey acknowledged. "It was hard work. Let's go have some coffee, and I'll tell you."

She'd picked up her symbol with no trouble—a good sign. She settled her attention on it, and waited. There'd been changes, she decided presently. It was as if a kind of life were seeping into the symbol, accumulating there. Another good sign. No need to push it now; she was moving in the right direction.

That might have gone on about an hour. Physically Telzey was feeling a little uncomfortable by then, which again could be counted, technically, a good sign, though she didn't like it. There was a frequent shivering in her skin, moments when breathing seemed difficult, other manifestations of apprehension. What it meant was that she was getting close.

Then there was an instant when she wasn't close, but there. Or *it* was there. The symbol faded as what had been behind it came slowly through. This was no visualization, but reality as sensed by psi. It was the darkness, the cold, in the false emptiness. It simmered with silent power. It was eminently forbidding.

It was there—then it wasn't there. It seemed to have become nonexistent.

But she needed no symbols to return to it now. What she had contacted, she could contact again. It was in her memory; and memory was a link. She could draw herself back to it.

She did, quickly lost it once more. Now there were two links. All she needed was patience.

Any feeling of passing time, all awareness of the room about her, of the chair in which she sat, even of her body, was gone. She was mind, in the universe of mind where she moved and searched, tracing the thing she had contacted, finding it, establishing new connections between herself and it. She lost it again and again, but each time it was easier to find, less difficult to hold. It was a great fish, and she a tiny fisherman, not fastening the fish to herself, but herself to the fish. Finally, the connection was stable, unchanging. When she was sure of that, she broke it. She could resume it whenever she chose.

At that point, she became conscious of the other reality, of her physical self and her surroundings.

And—once more—of having uninvited company.

This time, she ignored the presence. It faded quietly from her awareness as she opened her eyes, sat up in the armchair. . . .

"I think we're almost there," she told Trigger. "The thing's a structure, a psi structure. It's what the Service xenos found and tried to probe. And I can believe it bounced them—it's really charged up!"

"You're going to try to probe it?" Trigger asked.

Telzey nodded. "I'll have to. There's been no mind trace of the Siren, so that structure must act as its shield. I'll have to try to work through it. How, I won't know till I find out what it's like." She was silent a moment. "If it bounces me, too, I don't know what else we can do," she said. "But we'll start worrying about that then. I do have very good shields. And if I can get one solid contact with the Siren mind, we may have the problem solved. Unless they're basically murderous, of course. But I agree with you that they don't really seem to be that."

There were other factors involved. But that was still nothing to talk to Trigger about. "So everything's set up for the probe now," Telzey concluded. "Next time I'll try it. But I want to be a lot fresher for that, so it won't be tonight. We'll see how I feel tomorrow."

They turned in early. Telzey fell into sleep at once like drifting deep, deep down through a cool dark quiet sea. . . . Some time later then, she found herself standing in the Siren's container.

It wasn't exactly the container, though there was a shadowy indication of its walls in the distance. A kind of cold desert stretched out about her, and she stood at the base of the Siren.

A Siren which twisted enormously up into an icy sky, gigantic, higher than a mountain, huge limbs writhing. A noise like growing thunder was in the air; the desert sand shook under her, and her feet were rooted immovably in the sand. Then she saw that the Siren was tilting, falling toward her, would crush her. She heard herself screaming in terror.

She awoke.

She sat up in bed, breathing in quick short gasps. She looked around the dark room, reached for the light switch. As she touched it, light blazed in the hall beyond the door. "Trigger?" she called.

From the direction of Trigger's room came a shaky, "Yes?"

"Wait a moment!" Telzey climbed out of bed, started toward the door. Trigger met her there, robe wrapped around her, face pale, hair disheveled. "What's the matter?" Telzey asked.

Trigger tried to smile. "Had a dream—a nightmare .Whew! Going down to the kitchen for some hot milk to settle myself." She laughed unsteadily.

"A nightmare?" Telzey stared at her. "Wait—I'll come along."

They'd had the same dream. A dream apparently identical in all respects, except that in Trigger's dream, it was Trigger who was about to be crushed by the toppling monster Siren. Sitting in the kitchen, sipping their hot milk, they discussed it, looking at each other with uncertain eyes. Something had come into their minds as they slept—

"That Old Galactic shield of yours," Telzey pointed out, "is supposed to keep anything from reaching your subconscious mind processes—which includes the dream mechanisms."

Trigger gave her a startled glance.

"Unless I allow it!" she said. "And I think I did allow it."

"What?"

Trigger nodded, frowned, trying to remember. "I was half asleep," she said slowly. "Something seemed to be telling me to dissolve the shield. So I did."

"Why?"

Trigger shrugged helplessly. "It *seemed* perfectly all right! I wasn't surprised or alarmed—not until I started dreaming." She reflected, shook her head. "That's all I remember. I suppose there was another of those ghost structures floating around?"

Telzey nodded. "Probably." She couldn't recall anything that had happened before she started dreaming. "Some general impression—warning, threat," she said. "With a heavy fear charge."

"How could we have turned that into the same dream?"

Telzey said, "We didn't. Your mind was wide open. I'm a telepath." A dream could be manufactured in a flash, from whatever material seemed to match the impulse that induced it. "One of us whipped up the dream," she said. "The other shared it. We came awake almost at once then."

"That Siren," said Trigger after a moment, "really doesn't want to be probed."

"No, not at all. And it may be aware that I've got as far as its shield."

Two other psi minds around here, Telzey thought, should also be aware of that fact. The Psychology Service would hardly be trying to discourage her from the probe. But the observer the Old Galactics had left planted in the Siren might have some reason for doing it—and might have the ability to induce a warning nightmare. She wished she had some clue to the interest that ancient race was taking in the Sirens.

They finished their milk, sat talking a few minutes longer, decided there was no sense sitting up the rest of the night, and went back to bed. They left the light on in the hall outside their rooms. Somewhat to Telzey's surprise, she felt herself fall asleep again almost as soon as her head touched the pillow.

8

They awoke to a disagreeable day. The sky was gloomy; a wind blew in cold gusts about the house; and there were intermittent falls of rain. Breakfast was a silent affair, as each was withdrawn into her own thoughts. When they'd finished, Trigger went to a window and looked out. Telzey joined her. "Gruesome weather!" Trigger remarked darkly. "I feel depressed."

"So do I," said Telzey.

Trigger glanced at her. "You don't think it's the weather, do you?"

"No."

"It's in the house all around us," Trigger said, nodding. "I've felt it since I woke up. As if there were something unpleasant about that I might see or hear at any moment. More of that ghost stuff, isn't it?"

"Yes. It may wear off." But Telzey wasn't so sure it would wear off, and whether the entity behind the psi block wasn't reaching them now through the block. This was a subtler assault on their nerves, the darkening of mood, uneasiness, a prodding of anxieties—all too diffused to counter.

An hour later, it didn't seem to be wearing off. "You shouldn't try the probe while you're feeling like this, should you?" Trigger asked.

Telzey shook her head. "Not if I can help it—but I don't think I should put it off too long either."

They were vulnerable, and they'd stirred something up. Even left alone, it wouldn't necessarily settle down. It might keep undermining their defenses for hours, or shift to a more definite attack. The probe must be attempted, and soon. The Sirens existed, were an unpredictable factor; something had to be done. If she waited, she might be reduced to incapability. That could be the intention.

"Let's go outside and tramp around a while," Trigger said. "Maybe it will cheer us up. I usually like a good rainy day, really."

They donned rain capes and boots, went down to the lake. But the walk didn't cheer them up. The wind stirred the cold lake surface, soughed through the trees about them. The sky seemed to be growing darker; and the notion came to Telzey that if she looked closely enough, she'd be able to make out the giant Siren of their dream writhing among distant clouds. She stopped short, caught Trigger by the arm.

"This isn't doing any good!" she said. "It's focused on us, and we're dragging it around with us here. Let's go back, pick up swim gear, and clear out! I know a beach where it won't be rainy and cold. We can be there in an hour."

They sped south in the Cloudsplitter, came down on a beach lying golden and hot under a nearly cloudless sky. The wind that swept it was a fresh and happy one. They swam and tumbled in the surf, spirits lifting by the minute. They came out and sunned, talked and laughed, swam again, collected a troop of bronzed males, let themselves be taken to lunch, shook off the troop, fled fifty miles east along the beach, went back to the water for a final dip where breakers rose high, and emerged exhausted and laughing ten minutes later. "*Now* let's go tackle that Siren!"

They flew north again, dropping down at a town en route to buy two tickets to the currently most popular live show in Orado City. Just what would happen when the probe began seemed a rather good question. Enough had happened, at any rate, to make them feel the Malions shouldn't be anywhere in the area at the time. They stopped off at the caretaker's house, explained they'd intended taking in the show that night, but found they couldn't make it; so there were two expensive tickets on hand which shouldn't go to waste. . . . Ezd and wife were on their way to Orado City thirty minutes later.

Parked at the northern end of the grounds, Telzey and Trigger watched the caretakers leave. The Cloudsplitter lifted then, slid down into the carport of the summer house. They went in by a side entrance.

The house was quiet. If anything had taken note of their return, it gave no indication. They got arranged quickly in the study. Trigger would be sitting in on this session. The finicky part of the work was done; someone else's presence, the subtle whisper of half-caught surface thoughts and emotional flickerings nearby when her sensors were tuned fine, could no longer be a distraction to Telzey. And company would be welcome to both of them now. Trigger took a chair to the right of the one Telzey had been using, a dozen feet away. "Ready?" Telzey asked from beside the Siren container.

Trigger settled herself. "When you are."

Telzey switched off the psi block. Something came into the study then. Telzey glanced at Trigger. No, Trigger hadn't noticed. Telzey went slowly to her chair, sat down.

The presence was back. *That* didn't surprise her.

But Trigger . . .

She looked over at Trigger, Trigger gave her a sober smile. There was alert intelligence in her expression, along with concern she wasn't trying to hide. Trigger, undeniably, was in that chair, aware and awake. But in a sense she'd vanished a moment ago. The normal tiny stirrings of mind, of individuality, had ceased. There was stillness now, undisturbed.

Telzey slid a probe toward the stillness. It didn't seem to touch anything, but it was stopped. She drew it back.

A shield of totally unfamiliar type. Trigger evidently didn't realize it was there. But it sealed her off from outside influences like indetectable heavy armor.

Things had begun to add up. . . .

Telzey checked her own safeguards briefly. Mind screens which might be the lightest of veils, meant only to obscure her from psi senses while she peered out, so to speak, between them. Or, on other occasions, tough and resilient shields which had turned the sharpest probe she'd ever encountered and held up under ponderous onslaughts of psi energy. They could shift in an instant from one extreme to the other. Sometimes, though rarely now, they disappeared completely.

She restored contact—and it was back at once before her: the cold darkness, the emptiness that wasn't empty, the sense of forbidding, repelling power. She scanned cautiously along the impression but could make out no more about it than before.

So then the initial probe! A sensing psi needle reached, touched, drove in, withdrew. As it withdrew, something wrenched briefly and violently at Telzey.

She waited. The xenotelepathic faculty was an automatic one, operating in subconscious depths beyond her reach. She didn't know why it did what it did. But when she touched an alien mind, it began transforming alien concepts to concepts sufficently human in kind so that she understood them; and if she wanted to talk to that mind, it turned her concepts into ones the alien grasped. Usually the process was swift; within a minute or two there might be the beginnings of understanding.

No understanding came here. Her screens had gone tight as something gripped and twisted her. When she relaxed them deliberately again, nothing else happened.

A deeper probe then. She launched it, braced for the mental distortion.

It came. The shields stiffened, damping it, but she had giddy feelings of being dragged sideways, stretched, compressed. And the probe was being blocked. She drew it back. Strangeness writhed for a moment among her thoughts and was gone. Echo, at last, of alien mind—of the mind that wanted no contact!

The sense of violent distortion ended almost as soon as her probe withdrew. The dark lay before her again, sullen and re-pelling. A psi device, assembled by mind. A shield, a barrier. A formidable one. But she'd touched for a moment the fringes of the alien mind concealed by the barrier, and now contact with it, whether it wanted contact or not, might be very close. She'd have to do more than she'd done. She decid-ed to trust her shields.

She paused then, at a new awareness.

She wasn't alone. The presence had followed. More than a presence now. Mind, human mind, behind heavy shielding.

"What do you want?" Telzey asked.

Thought replied. "After you make the contact, you may need support."

She would. "Can you give it?"

"I believe so. Be ready!" The impression ended.

Telzey moved in her shields toward the dark barrier, reached it. The barrier awoke like a rousing beast. Her probe stabbed out, hard and solid. The barrier shook at her savage-ly, and mind-strangeness flickered again through her thoughts. She caught it, tagged it, felt incomprehensibility and an icy deadliness in the instant before it was gone. Now there had been contact—a thread of psi remained drawn between her-self and the alien mind, a thin taut line which led through the barrier. Following the line, she moved forward into the bar-rier, felt a madness of power surge up about her.

"Link with me quickly before—"

Vast pressures clamped down. Telzey and the other spun together through the thunders of chaos.

She'd joined defenses before the barrier struck. With whom, she didn't know, and there was no time just now to find out. But she'd felt new strength blend with hers in that moment, and the strength was very, very useful. For here was pounding confusion, a blurring and blackening of thought, a hideous distorting and twisting of emotion. The barrier was trying to eject her, force her back, batter her into helplessness. It was like moving upstream through raging and shifting cur-rents.

But the double shield absorbed it. And her psi line held.
For a time she wasn't sure she was moving at all through the
psi barrier's frenzies. Then she knew again that she was—

9

She was lying in bed in a darkened room and didn't have to
open her eyes to know it was her bedroom in the summer
house. She could sense its familiar walls and furnishings about
her. How she'd got there, she didn't know. Her mind screens
were closed; not drawn into a tight shield, but closed. Automatic precautionary procedure.

Precaution against what?

She didn't know that either.

Something evidently had happened. She felt very unpleas-
antly weak; and it wasn't the weakness of fatigued muscles.
Most of her strength seemed simply absent. There were no indications of physical damage otherwise. But her mental condition was deplorable! What had knocked out her memory?

The answer came slowly.

The Hana had knocked out her memory.

With that, it was all back. Telzey lay quiet, reflecting. That
incredible species! Waiting on the three worlds they'd filled
wherever they could grow, worlds transformed into deadly psi
forts—waiting for the return of an enemy they'd fought, how
long ago? Fifty thousand human years? A hundred thousand?

They'd been convinced the Veen would be back and attempt again to enslave or destroy them. And they'd been
ready to receive the Veen. What giant powers of attack and
defense they'd developed in that long waiting while their
minds lay deeply hidden! When an occasional psi entity began
to search them out, it was hurled back by the reef of mon-
strous energies they'd drawn about themselves. None had ever
succeeded in passing that barrier.

Until we did, Telzey thought.

They had; and the Hana mind, nakedly open, immensely
powerful, believing they were Veen who had penetrated its

defenses, began killing them. They'd lasted a while, under that double shield. They couldn't have lasted very long even so, because life was being drained from them into the Hana mind in spite of the shield; but there was time enough for Telzey's concept transforming process to get into operation. Then the Hana realized they weren't Veen, weren't enemies, didn't intend to attack it; and it stopped killing them.

Things had begun to get rather blurred for Telzey around then. But she'd picked up some additional details—mostly about the other who'd come through the barrier with her.

She relaxed her screens gradually. As she'd suspected, that other one was in the room. She opened her eyes, sat up unsteadily in bed, turned on the room lights.

Pilch sat in a chair halfway across the room, watching her. "I thought you'd come awake," she remarked.

Telzey settled back on the bed. "How's Trigger?"

"Perfectly all right. Asleep at present. She was behind a rather formidable shield at the time of contact."

"The Old Galactic's," said Telzey.

"Yes."

"What was *it* doing here—in the Hana?"

"A precaution the Old Galactics decided on after they realized what the Hana was," Pilch said. "If our psi investigations failed and the Hana began to cut loose, it would have died on the physical side. They have fast methods."

Telzey was silent a moment. "As I remember it," she said then, "you weren't in much better shape than I was when I passed-out."

"True enough," agreed Pilch. "We were both in miserable shape, more than half dead. Fortunately, I'm good at restoring myself. At that, it took me several days to get back to par."

"Several days?"

"It's been ten days since you made the contact," Pilch told her.

"Ten days!" Startled, Telzey struggled back up to a sitting position.

"Relax," said Pilch. "No one's missed you. Your family is under the impression you're vacationing around, and it won't occur to the caretakers to come near the house until we're ready to let them resume their duties. Which will be quite soon. I know you still feel wrung out, but you've been gaining ground very rapidly tonight. A few more hours will see you back to normal health. That was no ordinary weakness."

Telzey studied her thoughtfully.

"You use anyone about any way you like, don't you?" she said.

"You, too, have been known to use people, Telzey Amberdon!" Pilch remarked. "You and Trigger, in your various ways, share the quality of being most effective when thrown on your own resources. It seemed our best chance, and it was. None of our xenos could have done precisely what you did at the critical moment, and I'm not at all sure the contact could have been made in any other manner."

She glanced at the watch on her wrist, stood up and came over to the bed.

"Now you're awake and I'm no longer needed here. I'll be running along," she said. "Trigger can fill you in. If there's some specific question you'd like me to answer, go ahead."

"There's one question," Telzey said. "How old are you, Pilch?"

Pilch smiled. "Never you mind how old I am."

"You were there before they founded the Federation," Telzey said reflectively.

"If you saw that," said Pilch, "you've also seen that I helped found the Federation. And that I help maintain it. You might keep it in mind. Any time a snip of a psi genius can be useful in one of my projects, I'll use her."

Telzey shook her head slightly. "I don't think you'll use me again."

Pilch's knowing gray eyes regarded her a moment. Then Pilch's hand reached down and touched her cheek. Something like a surge of power flowed through Telzey and was absorbed. She blinked, startled.

Pilch smiled.

"We'll see, little sister! We'll see!" she said.

Then she was gone.

"Are you angry with her?" Trigger asked, an hour later, perched on the edge of Telzey's bed while they both took cautious sips from cups of very hot broth. It was early morning now, and they were alone in the house. The Hana and the Old Galactic had left with Pilch's people days ago, and Trigger had gathered they were going first to bring the news that the Veen War was over to the other Hanas currently in Hub laboratories. Afterward, they'd all be off together to the Hana planets to make arrangements which would avoid further problems.

Telzey shook her head.

"I'll forgive her this time," she said. "She took a chance on her own life helping me get through the Hana shield, and she knew it. Then she seems to have spent around a week of her time here, to make sure I'd recover."

Trigger nodded. "Yes, she did. You were looking pretty dead for a while, Telzey! They said you'd be all right, but I wasn't at all certain. Then Pilch appeared and took over, and you started to pick right up." She sighed. "Pilch has her ways!"

Telzey sipped her broth meditatively. The Hanas hadn't been the only ones who'd had trouble with the Veen. It appeared that conflict wasn't much more than a minor skirmish on the fringes of the ancient war which blazed through the empire of the Old Galactics and destroyed it, before the survivors of those slow-moving entities brought their own weapons into full play and wiped out the Veen. "The Old Galactics weren't too candid with you either, were they?" she said.

"No, they weren't," said Trigger. She regarded Telzey soberly. "It looks as though we got a bit involved in galactic politics for a while!"

Telzey nodded. "And I personally plan to keep out of galactic politics in the future!"

"Same here," Trigger agreed. "It doesn't—" She raised her head quickly as the ComWeb chimed in the hall. "Well, well! We seem to have been restored to the world! Wonder who it is. . . ."

She hurried from the room, came back shortly, smiling. "That Pilch!"

"Who was it?"

"Ezd Malion. Calling to say he was going to town early and did we want any groceries."

"No idea that it's been ten days since he talked to us last?" asked Telzey.

"None whatever! He's just picking up where he was told to leave off."

Telzey nodded.

"That's about what we'll be doing," she said. "But at least we know we're doing it."

Company Planet

1

Fermilaur was famous both as the leading body remodeling center of the Hub and as a luxurious resort world which offered relaxation and scenery along with entertainment to fit every taste, from the loftiest to the most depraved. It was only three hours from Orado, and most of Telzey's friends had been there. But she'd never happened to get around to it until one day she received a distress call from Fermilaur.

It came from the mother of Gikkes Orm. Telzey learned that Gikkes, endowed by nature with a pair of perfectly sound and handsome legs, had decided those limbs needed to be lengthened and reshaped by Fermilaur's eminent cosmetic surgeons if she was ever to find true happiness. Her parents, who, in Telzey's opinion, had even less good sense than Gikkes, had let her go ahead with it, and her mother had accompanied her to Fermilaur. With the legs remodeled according to specification, Gikkes had discovered that everything else about her now appeared out of proportion. Unable to make up her mind what to do, she bacame greatly upset. Her mother, equally upset, equally helpless, put in an interstellar call to Telzey.

Having known Gikkes for around two years, Telzey wasn't surprised. Gikkes didn't quite rate as a full friend, but she wasn't a bad sort even if she did get herself periodically into problem situations from which somebody else had to extricate her. Telzey decided she wouldn't mind doing it again. While about it, she should have time for a look at a few of Fermilaur's unique restructuring institutions and other attractions.

Somewhat past the middle of the night for that locality, she checked in at a tourist tower not far from the cosmetic center where the Orms were housed. She'd heard that Fermilaur used resort personnel to advertise its remodeling skills, the general note being that having oneself done over was light-hearted fashion fun and that there was nothing to worry about because almost any cosmetic modification could be reversed if the client wished it. The staff of the tower's reception lobby confirmed the report. They were works of art, testimonials to the daring inventiveness of Fermilaur's beauty surgeons. Telzey's room reservation was checked by a slender goddess with green-velvet skin, slanted golden eyes without detectable pupils, and a shaped scalp crest of soft golden feathers which shifted dancingly with each head motion. She smiled at Telzey, said, "May I suggest the services of a guide, Miss Amberdon?"

Telzey nodded. "Yes, I'll want one." There were no cities, no townships here. The permanent population was small, mostly involved with the tourist trade and cosmetic institutions, and its maintenance systems were underground, out of sight. Much of the surface had been transformed into an endlessly flowing series of parks in which residential towers and resort and remodeling centers stood in scenic isolation. Traffic was by air, and inexperienced visitors who didn't prefer to drift about more or less at random were advised to employ guides.

The goddess beckoned to somebody behind Telzey's back.

"Uspurul is an accredited COS Services guide and thoroughly familiar with our quadrant," she informed Telzey. "I'm sure you'll find her very satisfactory."

Uspurul was a quite small person, some four inches shorter than Telzey, slender in proportion. Like the receptionist, she looked like something COS Services might have conjured up out of exotic mythologies. Her pointed ears were as expressively mobile as a terrier's; a silver horse's tail swished about with languid grace behind her. The triangular face with its huge dark eyes and small delicate nose was unquestionably beautiful but wasn't human. It wasn't intended to be. She might have been a charming toy, brought to life.

Which was all very well, as far as Telzey was concerned. More important seemed a shadowy swirl of feeling she'd sensed as Uspurul came up to the reception desk—a feeling

which didn't match in the least the engaging friendliness of
the toy woman's smile. It wasn't exactly malice. More something like calculating cold interest, rather predatory. Telzey
took note of nuances in the brief conversation that followed,
decided the two were, in fact, more anxious to make sure
she'd employ Uspurul as guide than one should expect.

Somewhere else, that could have been a danger signal. A
sixteen-year-old with a wealthy family made a tempting target
for the criminally inclined. The resort world, however, had
the reputation of being almost free of professional crime.
And, in any case, it shouldn't be difficult to find out what this
was about—she'd discovered during the talk that Uspurul's
mind appeared to be wide open to telepathic probing.

"Why not have breakfast with me in my room tomorrow?"
she said to the guide. "We can set up a schedule then." And
she could ferret out at her leisure the nature of the interest the
remodeled myths seemed to take in her.

They settled on the time, and Telzey was escorted to her
room. She put in a call to Mrs. Orm from there, learned that
Gikkes would be in treatment at the main center of Hute
Beauticians during the early part of the morning and was anxious to see Telzey and get her opinion of the situation immediately afterward. Mrs. Orm having succeeded in transferring
the responsibility for decisions to somebody else, appeared
much less distraught.

Telzey opened one of her suitcases, got out a traveler's lock
and attached it to the door of the room, which in effect weld-
ed the door to the adjoining wall. The only thing anyone trying to get in without her cooperation could accomplish was to
wake up half the tower level. She continued unpacking reflectively.

Fermilaur didn't have a planetary government in the usual
sense. It was the leasehold of COS, the association of cosme-
tologists which ran the planet. Its citizen-owners, set up in a
tax-free luxury resort and getting paid for it, had reason to be
happy with the arrangement, and could have few inducements
to dabble in crime. The Hub's underworld reputedly had its
own dealings with COS—bodies, of course, could be restruc-
tured for assorted illegal purposes. But the underworld didn't
try to introduce its usual practices here. COS never denied reports that criminal pros found attempting to set up shop on

the leasehold vanished into its experimental centers. Apparently, not many cared to test the validity of the reports.

Hence, no crime, or almost no crime. And crime of the ordinary sort hardly could be involved in the situation. The receptionist and the elfin guide never had seen her before. But they did seem to have recognized her by name, to have been waiting, in fact, for her to show up.

Telzey sat down on the edge of the bed.

The two were COS employees. If anyone had an interest in her here, it should be COS.

The tower reservation had been made in her name five hours ago on Orado. Five hours was plenty of time for a good information service to provide inquirers with the general background of the average Federation citizen. Quite probably, COS had its own service and obtained such information on every first-time visitor to Fermilaur. It could be useful in a variety of ways.

The question was what might look interesting enough in her background to draw COS's attention to her. It wasn't that the Amberdon family had money. Almost everybody who came here would meet that qualification. There were, Telzey decided, chewing meditatively on her lower lip, only two possible points of interest she could think of at the moment. And both looked a little improbable.

Her mother was a member of the Overgovernment. Conceivably, that could be of significance to COS. At present, it was difficult to see why it should be.

The other possibility seemed even more remote. Information services had yet to dig up the fact that Telzey Amberdon was a telepath, a mind reader, a psi, competent and practicing. She knew that, because if they ever did dig it up, she'd be the first to hear. She had herself supplied regularly with any datum added to her available dossiers. Of the people who were aware she was a psi, only a very few could be regarded as not being completely dependable. Unfortunately, there were those few. It was possible, though barely so, that the item somehow had got into COS's files.

She could have a problem then. The kind of people who ran COS had to be practical and hardheaded. Hardheaded, practical people, luckily, were inclined to consider stories about psis to be at least ninety-nine percent superstitious nonsense. However, the ones who didn't share that belief sometimes reacted undesirably. They might reflect that a real psi, competent, practicing, could be eminently useful to them.

Or they might decide such a psi was too dangerous to have around.

She'd walk rather warily tomorrow until she made out what was going on here! One thing, though, seemed reasonably certain—COS, whatever ideas it might have, wasn't going to try to break through the door to get at her tonight. She could use a few hours of rest.

She climbed into bed, turned over, and settled down. A minute or two later, she was alseep.

2

After breakfast, Telzey set off with Uspurul on a leisurely aircar tour of the area. She'd explained she'd be visiting an acquaintance undergoing treatment at Hute Beauticians later on, and then have lunch with another friend who'd come out from Orado with her. In the afternoon, she might get down finally to serious sightseeing.

With Uspurul handling the car and gossiping merrily away, Telzey could give her attention to opening connections to the guide's mind. As she'd judged, it was an easy mind to enter, unprotected and insensitive to telepathic probing. One fact was promptly established then, since it was pervasively present in Uspurul's thoughts. COS did, in fact, take a special interest in Telzey, but it wasn't limited to her. She had plenty of company.

The reason for the interest wasn't apparent. Uspurul hadn't wanted to know about it, hardly thought of it. The little female was a complex personality. She was twenty-two, had become a bondswoman four years earlier, selling her first contract to COS Services for the standard five-year short-term period. People who adopted bondservant status did it for a wide range of reasons. Uspurul's was that a profitable career could be built on bond contracts by one who went about it intelligently. She'd chosen her masters after careful deliberation.

On a world which sold luxury, those who served also lived in relative luxury, and as a COS guide she was in contact with influential and wealthy people who might be used for her further advancement. Her next contract owner wouldn't be COS. She was circumspect in her behavior. More was done on Fermilaur than cultivating an exclusive tourist trade and cosmetic clientele, and it wasn't advisable to appear inquisitive about the other things. COS didn't mind rumors about various barely legal or quite illegal activities in which it supposedly engaged; they titillated public interest and were good for business. But underlings who became too knowledgeable about such obscure matters could find it difficult to quit.

Uspurul intended to remain free to quit when her contract period ended. For the past year, she'd been on the fringes of something obscure enough. It had brought her a string of satisfactory bonuses, and there was nothing obviously illegal about what she did or COS Services did. As long as she avoided any indication of curiosity it seemed safe.

She still acted as guide. But she was assigned now only to female tourists who appeared to have no interest in making use of the remodeling facilities. Uspurul's assignment was to get them to change their minds without being obvious about it. She was skillful at that, usually succeeded. On a number of occasions when she hadn't succeeded, she'd been instructed to make sure the person in question would be at a certain place at a certain time. She'd almost always been able to arrange it.

Now she was using the morning's comfortable schedule to keep up a flow of the light general chatter through which she could most readily plant the right notions in a hesitant visitor's mind.

"I was thinking I might have a little remodeling myself while I was here," Telzey remarked, by and by. She took out a small mirror, looked into it critically, arching her brows. "Nothing very important really! But I could have my brows moved higher, maybe get the eyes enlarged." She clicked the mirror to an angle view, pushed back her hair on the left side. "And the ears, you see, could be set a little lower—and the least bit farther back." She studied the ear a moment. "What do you think of their shape?"

"Oh, I wouldn't have them change the *shape!*" said Uspurul, thinking cheerfully that here came an easy bonus! "But they might be a tiny bit lower. You're right about that."

Telzey nodded, put the mirror away. "Well, no rush about it. I'll be looking around a few days first."

"Someone like you doesn't really need remodeling, of course," Uspurul said. "But it is fun having yourself turned into exactly what you'd like to be! And, of course, it's always reversible."

"Hmmm," said Telzey. "They did a beautiful job on you. Did you pick it out for yourself?"

Uspurul twitched an ear, grinned impishly.

"I've wanted to do *that* since I was a child!" she confessed. "But, no—this was COS Services' idea. I advertise for the centers, you see. A twenty-two thousand credit job, if I had to pay for it. I'd be a little extreme for the Hub generally, of course. But it's reversible, and when I leave they'll give me any other modification I want within a four thousand credit range. That's part of my contract."

She burbled on. Telzey didn't have the slightest intention of getting remodeled, but she wanted Uspurul and COS Services to think she did until she was ready to ship out. It would keep the situation more relaxed.

It remained a curious situation. The people to whom Uspurul reported were satisfied if a visitor signed up for any kind of remodeling at all, even the most insignificant of modifications. That hardly looked like a simple matter of drumming up new business for the centers, while the special attention given some of those who remained disinterested was downright on the sinister side. The places to which Uspurul steered such tourists were always resort spots where there were a good many other people around, coming and going—places, in other words, where somebody could easily brush close by the tourist without attracting attention.

What happened there? Something perhaps in the nature of a hypno spray? Uspurul never saw what happened and didn't try to. When she parted company with the tourist that day, there'd been no noticable effects. But next day she'd be given a different assignment.

Of course, those people weren't disappearing. It wasn't *that* kind of situation. They weren't, by and large, the kind of people who could be made to vanish quietly. Presumably they'd been persuaded by some not too legal method to make a remodeling appointment, and afterward went on home like Uspurul's other clients. They might all go home conditioned to keep returning to Fermilaur for more extensive and expensive treatments; at the moment, that seemed the most probable explanation. But whatever the COS Services' operation was, Telzey reflected, she'd simply make sure she didn't get included in it. With Uspurul's mind open to her, that shouldn't be too difficult. Back on Orado then, she'd bring the matter to the attention of Federation authorities. Meanwhile she might run across a few other open minds around here who could tell her more than Uspurul knew.

The man she was meeting for lunch—a relative on her mother's side—was an investigative reporter for one of the newscast systems. Keth had his sharp nose into many matters, and exposing rackets was one of his specialties. He might be able to say what this was about, but the difficulty would be to explain how she'd come by her information without mentioning telepathy. Keth didn't know she was a psi. Nor could she do her kind of mental research on him—she'd discovered on another occasion that he was equipped with a good solid commercial mind shield. Keth doubted that anyone could really see what was in another person's mind, but he took precautions anyway.

The remodeling counselors at the Hute Beauticians center had told Gikkes Orm quite candidly that if she was to be equipped with the leg type she wanted, overall body modification were indicated to maintain an aesthetic balance. Gikkes hadn't believed it. But now the cosmetic surgeons had given her a pair of long, exquisitely molded legs, and it seemed the counselors were right.

The rest of her didn't fit.

"Just look at those shoulders!" she cried, indicating one of two life-sized models which stood against the far wall of the room. They showed suggested sets of physical modifications which might be performed on Gikkes. "I love the legs! But—"

"Well, you might be a little, uh, statuesque," Telzey acknowledged. She studied the other model. Sinuous was the word for that one. A dancer's body. "But, Gikkes, you'd look great either way, really! Especially as the slinky character!"

"It wouldn't be *me!*" Gikkes wailed. "And how much work do you think I'd have to put in to *stay* slinky then? You know I'm not an athletic type."

"No, I guess you're not," Telzey said. "When did you first get the idea that you wanted your legs changed?"

It appeared Gikkes had been playing around with the notion for several years, but it was only quite recently that it had begun to seem vital to her. It was her own idea, however—not an obsession planted on a previous trip to Fermilaur. Telzey had been wondering about that. The solution shouldn't be too difficult. Off and on for some while, Telzey had made use of suitable occasions to nudge Gikkes in the general direction of rationality. It had to be done with care because Gikkes wasn't too stable. But she had basic intelligence and, with some unnoticed guidance, was really able to handle most of her problems herself and benefit from doing it. Telzey picked up the familiar overall mind patterns now, eased a probe into the unhappy thought muddle of the moment, and presently began her nudging. Gikkes went on talking.

Twenty minutes later, she said ruefully, "So I guess the whole remodeling idea was a silly mistake! The thing to do, of course, is to have them put me back exactly as I was."

"From all you've told me," Telzey agreed, "that does make sense."

Mrs. Orm was surprised but relieved when informed of her daughter's decision. The Hute staff wasn't surprised. Remodeling shock and reversal requests weren't infrequent. In this case, reversal was no problem. Gikkes experiment in surgical cosmetology probably had reduced her life expectancy by an insignificant fraction, and the Orm family was out a good deal of money, which it could afford. Otherwise, things would be as before.

A level of the Hute center restaurant was on Keth Deboll's private club circuit, which in itself guaranteed gourmet food. It was a quietly formal place where the employees weren't trying to look like anything but people. Keth's bony inquisitive face, familiar to newsviewers over a large section of the Hub, presumably didn't go unrecognized here, but nobody turned to stare. He deliberated over the menu, sandy brows lifting in abrupt interest now and then, and ordered for both of them, rubbing his palms together.

"You'll like it," he promised.

She always did like what Keth selected, but this time she barely tasted what she put in her mouth, as she chewed and swallowed. He'd mentioned that top COS executives patronized the place, and that he rather expected to be meeting someone before lunch was over.

She'd been wondering how she could get close enough to some top COS executive to start tapping his mind. . . .

She was sliding out discreet probes before Keth had placed his order. After the food came, only a fraction of awareness remained in her physical surroundings. Keth would eat in leisurely silent absorption until the edge was off his appetite, and she might have her contact made by that time.

Several minds in the vicinity presently seemed as open to contact as Uspurul's. None of them happened to be a COS executive. Something else was in the vicinity—seven or eight mind shields. Unusual concentration of the gadgets! Her probes slipped over them, moved on, searching—

"You might get the opportunity," Keth's voice was saying. "Here comes a gentleman who could arrange it for you."

Awareness flowed swiftly back to the outer world as she reoriented herself between one moment and the next. Keth had reached the point where he didn't mind talking again, had asked—what? Ah, yes, had asked what plans she had for the day. She'd responded, automatically, that she was hoping to get a look at some of Fermilaur's less publicized projects. . . . Who could arrange it?

She looked around. A handsome, tall, strong-faced man was coming toward their table. On his right shoulder perched a small creature with blue and white fur, adorned with strings of tiny sparkling jewels. The man's dark eyes rested on Telzey as he approached. He nodded to her, smiled, pleasantly, looked at Keth.

"Am I intruding?" It was a deep, soft-toned voice.

"Not at all," Keth told him. "We're almost finished—and I'd intended trying to get in touch with you during the afternoon. Telzey, this is Chan Osselin. He handles publicity for COS and incidentally owns Hute Beauticians. . . . Telzey Amberdon, an old friend. We came out from Orado together. If you have the time, join us."

Osselin drew a chair around and sat down. His scalp hair was short, deep black, like soft animal fur. Telzey wondered whether it was a product of remodeling, felt rather certain then that it wasn't. The small animal on his shoulder stared at Telzey out of large pale eyes, yawned and scratched a rounded ear with a tiny clawed finger. The stringed jewels decorating it flashed flickering rainbows of fire.

"I heard of your arrival a few hours ago," Osselin said. "Here on Adacee business?"

Keth shrugged. "Always on Adacee business."

"Um. Something specific?"

"Not so far. Something new, unpublicized, sensational."

Osselin looked reflective. "Sensational in what way?"

"Questionable legality wouldn't have to be part of it," Keth said. "But it would help. Something with shock effect. None of your pretty things."

"So COS is to be exposed again?" Osselin seemed unruffled.

"With some new angle," said Keth. "On some new issue."

"Well," Osselin said, "I'm sure it can be arranged. . . ."

Telzey, absently nibbling the last crumbs of her dessert, drew back her attention from what was being said. She'd known Chan Osselin's name as soon as she saw him. She'd seen him before as an image in Uspurul's mind. One of COS's top men. Uspurul wouldn't willingly have brought herself to the attention of someone like Osselin. People of that kind were to be avoided. They had too much power, were too accustomed to using it without hesitation or scruple.

There was no trace of the dead, psi-deadening, effect of a mind shield about Osselin—

Telzey reached out toward the deep sound of his voice, paying no attention to the words, groping cautiously for some wash of thought which might be associated with the voice.

She had no warning of any kind. A psi hammer slammed down on her, blacking out her vision, leaving her shaken and stunned.

3

She drew in a slow, cautious breath. Her psi screens had locked belatedly into a hard shield; another assault of that kind could have no great effect on her now. But none came.

She realized she'd lowered her head in protective reflex. Her hair hid her face, and the voices of the men indicated they weren't aware that anything in particular had happened. Vision began to return. The section of the tabletop before her grew clear, seemed to sway about in short semicircles. A last wave of giddiness and nausea flowed over her and was gone. She'd be all right now. But that had been close—

She kept her face turned away as she reached for her bag. The makeup cassette showed she'd paled, but it wasn't too noticable. Listening to a thin, angry whistling nearby, she touched herself up, put the cassette away, and finally raised her head.

The furry thing on Osselin's shoulder stared at her. Abruptly it produced its whistling sounds again, bobbing up and down. Osselin stroked it with a finger. It closed its eyes and subsided. He smiled at Telzey.

"It gets agitated now and then about strangers," he remarked.

She smiled back. "So it seems. What do you call it?"

"It's a yoli. A pet animal from Askanam. Rare even there, from what I've been told. This one came to me as a gift."

"Supposed to be a sort of living good luck charm, aren't they?" said Keth.

"Something like that. Faithful guardians who protect their master from evil influences." Osselin's dark eyes crinkled genially at Telzey. "I can't vouch for their effectiveness—but I do seem to remain undisturbed by evil influences! Would you care to accompany us to a few of the specialized labs a little later, Miss Amberdon? You should find them interesting."

Keth was to be shown a few projects COS didn't talk about otherwise, which might give him the kind of story he wanted. They preferred that to having him dig around on Fermilaur on his own. She told Osselin she'd be delighted to go along.

The yoli appeared to be falling asleep, but she sensed its continuing awareness of her. A psi guard—against psis. Its intelligence seemed on the animal level. She couldn't make out much more about it, and didn't care to risk trying at present. It probably would react as violently to an attempted probe of its own mind as to one directed against its master.

And now she might be in personal danger. The number of shields she'd touched here suggested some sophistication in psi matters. Ordinarily it wouldn't disturb her too much. Mechan-

ical anti-psi devices could hamper a telepath but weren't likely
to lead to the detection of one who'd gained some experience,
and other telepaths rarely were a problem. The yoli's psi
senses, however, had been a new sort of trap; and she'd
sprung it. She had to assume that Osselin knew of his pet's
special quality and what its behavior just now signified. A
man like that wasn't likely to be indifferent to the discovery
that someone had tried to reach his mind. And the yoli had
made it clear who it had been.

If she dropped the matter now, it wasn't likely that Osselin
would drop it. And she wouldn't know what he intended to do
then until it was too late. . . .

Some time later, as the tour of the special labs began, there
was an attention split. Telzey seemed aware of herself, or of
part of herself, detached, a short distance away. That part
gazed at the exhibits, smiled and spoke when it should, asked
questions about projects, said the right things—a mental device she'd worked out and practiced to mask the sleepy blank-
ness, the temporary unawareness of what was said and done,
which could accompany excessive absorption on the psi side.
On the psi side, meanwhile, she'd been carrying on a project
of her own which had to do with Osselin's yoli.

The yoli was having a curious experience. Shortly after Telzey and Keth rejoined Osselin, it had begun to pick up momentary impressions of another yoli somewhere about. Greatly intrigued because it had been a long time since it last encountered or sensed one of its kind, it started searching mentally for the stranger, broadcasting its species' contact signals.

Presently the signals were being returned, though faintly
and intermittently. The yoli's excitement grew. It probed farther and farther for the signals' source, forgetting now the telepath it had punished for trying to touch its master. And
along those heedlessly extended tendrils of thought, Telzey
reached delicately toward the yoli mind, touched it and melt-
ed into it, still unperceived.

It had taken time because she couldn't risk making the
creature suspicious again. The rest wasn't too difficult. The
yoli's intelligence was about that of a monkey. It had natural
defenses against being controlled by another's psi holds, and
Telzey didn't try to tamper with those. Its sensory centers
were open to her, which was all she needed. Using its own im-

pressions of how another yoli, a most desirable other yoli, would appear to it, she built up an illusion that it was in satisfying communication with such a one and left the image planted firmly in its mind along with a few other befuddling concepts. By that time, the yoli was no longer aware that she existed, much less of what she was up to.

Then finally she was able to turn her attention again to Osselin. Caution remained required, and she suspected she might be running short of time. But she could make a start.

The aircar floated three thousand feet above foggy valley lands—Fermilaur wilderness, tamed just enough to be safe for the tourist trade. Tongue tip between lips, Telzey blinked at the clouds, pondering a thoroughly ugly situation. There was a sparse dotting of other cars against the sky. One of them was trailing her; she didn't know which. It didn't matter.

She glanced impatiently over at the comm grille. Keth Deboll was in conference somewhere with Osselin. She'd left a message for him at his residential tower to call her car's number as soon as he showed up. She'd left word at her own tower to have calls from him transferred to the car. In one way or the other, she'd be in contact with him presently. Meanwhile she had to wait, and waiting wasn't easy in the circumstances.

Chan Osselin couldn't sense a telepathic probe. Except for that, she might have been defeated and probably soon dead. She'd found him otherwise a difficult mental type to handle. His flow of conscious thoughts formed a natural barrier; it had been like trying to swim against a current which was a little too strong. She kept getting pushed back while Osselin went on thinking whatever he was thinking, unaware of her efforts. She could follow his reflections but hadn't been able to get past them to the inner mind in the time she had available. . . . And then she'd been courteously but definitely dismissed. The guided tour was over, and the men had private business to discuss. Shortly after she left them, she'd lost her contact with Osselin.

She'd absorbed a good deal of scattered information by then, could begin fitting it together. As she did, the picture, looking bad enough to start with, got progressively worse—

Normally, even people who accepted that there might be an occasional mind reader around had the impression that telepathy couldn't pick up enough specific and dependable information to be a significant threat to their privacy. That might have been the attitude of the top men in COS up to a year ago. Unfortunately, very unfortunately for her, they'd had a genuine psi scare then. They spotted the psi and killed him, but when they realized how much he'd learned, that they almost hadn't found him out in time, they were shaken. Mind shields and other protective devices were promptly introduced. Osselin hated shields; like many others he found them as uncomfortable as a tight shoe. When an Askab lady provided him with a guard yoli, he'd felt it was safe to do without a shield.

He still felt safe personally. That wasn't the problem. COS had something going, a really important operation. Telzey had caught worried flashes about it, no more and not enough. The Big Deal was how Osselin thought of it. They couldn't afford the chance of having the Big Deal uncovered. Keth Deboll was a notoriously persistent and successful snoop; a telepathic partner would make him twice as dangerous. The fact that the two had appeared on Fermilaur together might have no connection with the Big Deal, but who could tell? COS was checking on both at present. If they couldn't be cleared, they'd have to be killed. Risky, but it could be arranged. It would be less risky, less suspicious, than carrying out a double mind-wipe and dumping them on some other world, which might have been an alternative in different circumstances.

And that was it! Telzey wet her lips, felt a chill quivering again through her nerves, a sense of death edging into the situation. She didn't see how they could be cleared. Neither did Osselin, but something might turn up which would make it unnecessary to dispose of them. The Amberdon girl's demise or disappearance shouldn't cause too much trouble, but Deboll was another matter. Too many people would start wondering whether he hadn't been on the trail of something hot on Fermilaur, what it could be. This would have to be *very* carefully handled! Meanwhile COS was taking no chances. Neither of the two would be allowed to leave the planet or get near an interstellar transmitter. If they made the attempt, they'd get picked up at once. Otherwise, they could remain at large, under surveillance, until the final decision was made. That should turn up any confederate they might have here.

The final decision was still some hours away. How many,

Telzey didn't know. Osselin hadn't known it yet. But not very many, in any case. . . .

Osselin himself might be the only way out of this. Their information on psis was limited; they thought of her only as a telepath, like the other one, and didn't suspect she could have further abilities which might endanger them. She had that advantage at present. Given enough time, she should be able to get Osselin under control. She'd considered trying to restore mental contact with him at long range, wherever he happened to be. But she wasn't at all certain she could do it, and the yoli made it too risky. Its hallucinations should be self-sustaining for some hours to come if nothing happened to disturb it seriously. She had to avoid disturbing it in resuming contact with Osselin, which meant working with complete precision. A fumble at long range could jolt the creature out of its dreams and into another defensive reaction.

She didn't know what effect that would have on Osselin, but at the very least it might give him the idea to equip himself with a mind shield as a further safeguard until they'd dealt with the telepath. She'd be stopped then.

She had to be *there*, with Osselin, to be sure of what she was doing. If she got in touch with him and told him she'd like to talk to him privately, he'd probably want to hear what she had to say. But he'd be suspicious, on guard. It would be easier for Keth to find a plausible reason for another meeting, easier if Keth was around to keep some of Osselin's attention away from her. . . . The comm grille burred. She gave a gasp of relief as her hand flicked out to switch it on.

4

Keth took a little convincing then. He'd set their aircar down on a grassy hillside, and they'd moved off until it was a hundred yards below them. He'd turned on this and that anti-snoop device. From eight feet away, their voices were an indistinguishable muddle of sound, their features blurred out.

"We can talk," he'd said.

Telzey talked. He listened, intent blue eyes blinking, face expressionless. Twice he seemed about to interject something, then let her go on. Finally he said, "Telzey, you're obviously not joking, and I don't believe you've suddenly become deranged. Did you ever try to read my mind?"

She nodded.

"Yes, once. Half a year ago. I thought you were up to something and wanted to find out what it was."

"Oh? What did you find?"

"That you use a mind shield, of course. I didn't waste any more time."

Keth grunted. "All right! You're a telepath. If the situation is what it looks like, we have a problem. The check on me won't tell COS anything. Adacee isn't leakproof, but all they'll learn there is what I told Osselin. I came to Fermilaur to get a good story. Nothing specific. Any story as long as it's good enough. Can they find anything in your background to confirm that you're a mind reader?"

Telzey shrugged, shook her head. "I've been careful. What there was has been pretty well covered up. It's very unlikely they'll find anything. The trouble is Osselin's already pretty well convinced of it—he goes by the yoli's psi sense. And, of course, they can't prove that I'm *not* one."

"No. Not without linking you into a lie detector system. If they go that far, they'll already have decided to go all the way with us. At any rate, they haven't made up their minds yet. I parted from Osselin on apparently friendly terms. If the verdict's favorable, nothing at all will have happened."

"Unless we try to reach a spaceport," Telzey said. "Or to get in touch with somebody somewhere else."

"Yes, they wouldn't allow that. And, of course, they can seal off the planet as far as we're concerned. In effect, they own it." Keth considered. "There's a man I might contact here, but that would only pull him into the trouble. How about other, uh, functional telepaths?"

Telzey shook her head.

"Starting cold, it probably would be hours before I located one. We don't have that much time. They mightn't want to help anyway. It could cost them *their* cover."

Keth rubbed his chin. "If it gets to the point of running, a space yacht might get us off."

"COS Services handles the yacht rentals," Telzey reminded him.

"Not what I was thinking of," Keth said. "Plenty of people come here in private yachts. Last year, I got out of a somewhat similar situation that way. It shouldn't be impossible to borrow one, but it probably wouldn't be easy." He reflected. "That Big Deal of COS—the story they think we might be snooping around here for? You got no clue from Osselin what that might be?"

She shook her head. "There's an awful lot of money involved, and there's something illegal about it. They'll protect it, whatever it takes. They think you might have picked up some clues to it somewhere and brought me to Fermilaur to help dig up more. But that's all I can say. Everything else connected with it was too blurred to make out."

"Finance, politics, business—the big money areas," Keth said, watching her. "Nothing about some secret Hub-wide system to gather hot inside information at top levels there."

Telzey stared at him. "Oh, my!" she said after a long moment.

Keth said, "You went white, Telzey. What is it?"

"That guide I had this morning! Uspurul." Telzey put her hand to her mouth. "I was reading *her* mind. There was something odd going on. I didn't think there was any connection, but I wanted to check with Uspurul again to be sure. I tried to get in touch with her an hour ago. COS Services said she was on another assignment, couldn't be reached."

"You don't think she's on another assignment?"

"Uh-uh! No. She didn't know it, but she's connected with their Big Deal! Hot inside information— When they started checking this afternoon on what I've been doing here since I landed, they'd have picked her up to see what a telepath could have got from her."

Keth said, "The kind of lie detector that pushes unconscious material to view. . . . So just what did you learn from her?"

Telzey recounted the essentials. Keth nodded slowly. He'd paled somewhat himself.

"That will have tipped the fat into the fire!" he said.

A secret Hub-wide information gathering system on the distaff side. . . .Wives, mistresses, daughters of the Federation's greats streamed in to Fermilaur. Were tagged on arrival, maneuvered into making a remodeling appointment if that hadn't been their intention.

"Anesthesia, unconsciousness, in-depth interrogation," Keth said. "Anything they know of significance is filed immediately. The ones who can be typed as foolproof COS agents and have sufficiently valuable connections go home under a set of heavy compulsions, go to work. When their work's done, they come back, get debriefed. Leaving no trace of what's happened, in case of subsequent checks. Yes, a big setup! COS's capital investment program should be spectacularly successful!"

Now and then suspicion might turn on an unwitting agent. When it happened, the agent appeared to go into amnesiac withdrawal and committed suicide at the first opportunity. It wasn't something the people involved would want to talk about. But there'd been such a case among Keth's acquaintances, and he'd learned of another very similar one, discovered both women had gone through remodeling centers on Fermilaur in recent months. It seemed worth following up. He'd come to Fermilaur to do it.

"I dislike turning my back on a story before it's in the bag," he said. "But I can pick this up at the other end now. We'd better get set to run while we can, Telzey! The decision they'll reach is to do us in. From their viewpoint, there won't be much choice."

"A yacht?" she said.

"Yes. Noticed a few boat parks while I was moving around this morning, and—"

"Keth, how much chance would we have of getting away?"

He hesitated, grimaced.

"It depends. Even odds perhaps, if we act now. Less if we wait."

She shook her head. "We can do better! Chan Osselin's really top man in COS, isn't he?"

Keth looked at her. "Yes. Barrand's president of the association. I've heard Osselin could have the job any time he wants. What he says pretty well goes anyway. Why?"

"You've got to think of some reason to see him again immediately, with me. I need more time to work on him, to really get into his mind."

"What will that do for us?"

"If I get through to him, Osselin will get us off Fermilaur,"

Telzey said. "He's in a better position to do it than anyone else."

Keth considered her.

"It seems you're something more than a telepath," he remarked.

"They don't know it."

"All right. How much time would you need?"

She shook her head.

"An hour—thirty minutes—twenty minutes—two hours . . . I don't know. It's always different, and Osselin isn't easy. But we'll have much better than even odds there!"

"Well, there's no need to arrange for a meeting," Keth said. He looked at his watch. "We've got a dinner appointment at Osselin's house two and a half hours from now, our local time. He emphasized that I was to bring my charming young friend along. Two people want to meet us. One's Barrand, the COS president I mentioned. The other's Nelt, vice-president and executive officer. They and Osselin are the trio that runs COS. Presumably the decision on what to do about us will be made at that time."

"Yes, probably," Telzey said. "But let's get there early, Keth."

"By about half an hour? I'm sure Osselin won't object. I've thought of further details about the projects he showed me that I'd like to discuss with him." He added as they turned back to the aircar, "But we're not scratching the space yacht idea just yet!"

"We're not?"

"No. COS *might* decide to lower the boom before we have a chance to sit down to dinner this evening. And you see, there're three special yacht types. Racing boats . . ."

The three yacht types had one thing in common: an identical means of emergency entry. It was designed for use in space but could be operated when the vessel was parked if one knew how. Keth did, though it wasn't general knowledge ."It's quick," he said. "We can do it from the car. Since we haven't spotted the people who are trailing us, they're doing it at a discreet distance. The chances are we'll be inside and going up before they realize what we're thinking about. So let's put in the next hour looking around for yachts like that! If the situation looks favorable, we'll snatch one."

Telzey agreed. Keth was an expert yachtsman.

It appeared, however, that no yachts in that category happened to be in the general area that day. After an hour, Telzey transferred her belongings to the residential tower where Keth was registered. It seemed better not to become separated now. They settled down to wait together until it would be time to go to Osselin's residence.

5

Osselin's yoli was still in timeless communion with the yoli of its dreams but beginning to show indications of uneasiness. The imagery had become static and patchy here and there. Telzey freshened it up. The yoli murmured blissfully, and was lost again.

Since their last meeting, Osselin had added a piece of pertinent equipment to his attire—a psi recorder, disguised as a watch and fastened by a strap to his brawny wrist. Its complex energies registered as a very faint burring along Telzey's nerves. She'd come across that particular type of instrument before. It was expensive, highly touted in deluxe gambling establishments and the like. It did, in fact, indicate any of the cruder manipulations of psi energy, which had earned it a reputation for reliability. One of its drawbacks was that it announced itself to sufficiently sensitive psis, a point of which the customers weren't aware. And here it was no real threat to Telzey. The psi flows she used in investigative work were well below such a device's registration levels.

Barrand and Nelt had showed up presently, bringing two stunning young women with them. The girls, to Telzey's satisfaction, were gaily talkative creatures. Barrand was short, powerfully built. Nelt was short and wiry. Both had mind shields. Both wore psi recorders of the same type as Osselin's, though theirs weren't in sight. And like Osselin they were waiting for the tactile vibrations from the recorders which would tell them that psi was being used.

So they weren't really sure about her.

She'd split her attention again. Keth knew about that now,

knew what to do to alert her if she didn't seem to be behaving in a perfectly normal manner. With suspicious observers on hand, that had seemed an advisable precaution. Keth and the ladies carried most of the conversation—the ladies perhaps putting up unwitting verbal screens for their escorts, as Keth was maintaining one to give Telzey as much freedom for her other activities as possible. Now and then she was aware that the COS chiefs studied her obliquely, somewhat as one might watch a trapped but not entirely predictable animal. The psi recorders remained inactive. She made progress along expanding lines with Osselin, sampled a series of dishes with evident apppreciation, joined occasionally in the talk—realized dinner was over.

"Of course, I want to see Sorem!" she heard herself say. "But what in the world is a guilt-smeller?"

Nelt's lovely companion made fluttering motions with tapered white hands. "I'll keep my eyes closed until he's gone again!" she said apprehensively. "I looked at him *once* with his helmet off! I had nightmares for a month."

The others laughed. Osselin reached around for the yoli, perched at the moment on the back of his chair. He placed it on his lap. "I'll keep my pet's eyes closed, too, while he's in the room," he said, smiling at Telzey. "It isn't easily frightened, but for some reason it's in deathly fear of Sorem. Guilt-smeller . . . well, Sorem supposedly has the ability to pick anyone with a strong feeling of guilty apprehension out of a group." He shrugged.

"He's unnatural," Nelt's lady told Telzey earnestly. "I don't care what they say—Sorem never was human! He couldn't have been."

"I might let him know your opinion of him," Barrand rumbled.

The girl paled in genuine fright. "Don't! I don't want him to notice me at all."

Barrand grinned. "You're in no danger—unless, of course, you have something to hide."

"Everybody has *something* to hide!" she protested. "I—" She broke off.

Faces turned to Telzey's right. Sorem, summoned unnoticed by Barrand, had come into the room. She looked around.

Sorem wore black uniform trousers and boots; a gun was

fastened to his belt. The upper torso was that of a powerful man, narrow at the waist, wide in the shoulders, with massively muscled arms and chest. It was naked, hairless, a lusterless solid black, looking like sculptured rock. The head was completely enclosed by a large snouted helmet without visible eye slits.

This figure came walking toward the table, helmet already turning slowly in Telzey's direction. In Osselin's mind, she had looked at the head inside the helmet. Black and hairless like the body, the head of an animal, of a huge dog, yellow-eyed and savage. Barrand's bodyguard—a man who'd liked the idea of becoming a shape of fear enough to undergo considerable risks in having himself transformed into one. The great animal jaws were quite functional. Sorem was a triumph of the restructuring artists' skills.

The recorders had indicated no stir of psi throughout dinner. But they thought that perhaps she simply was being cautious now. Sorem was to frighten her, throw her off guard, jolt her into some revealing psi response. So she would show fear —which mightn't be too difficult. Sorem's mind was equipped with a shield like his employer's, but a brutish mirth and cruelty washed through it as he made it plain his attention was on her. Telzey glanced quickly, nervously, around the table, looked back at him. Keth's face was intent; he didn't know what would happen, whether it wasn't their executioner who had been called into the room. Sorem came up, steps slowing, a stalking beast. Telzey stopped breathing, went motionless, staring up at him. Abruptly, the helmet was swept away; the dog head appeared, snarling jaws half open. The eyes glared into Telzey's.

The yoli squealed desperately, struggling under Osselin's hand.

There were violent surges of psi energy then. The yoli wasn't fully aware of what was happening, but a nightmare shape had loomed up in its dreams, and it wanted to get away. Telzey couldn't afford to let it wake up now, and didn't. The three psi recorders remained active for perhaps forty-five seconds. Then she'd wiped the fright impressions from the yoli's mind, made it forget why it had been frightened. . . .

"It must have recognized your creature by his scent," Osselin was saying. "I had its eyes covered."

He stroked the yoli's furry head. It still whimpered faintly but was becoming reabsorbed by its fantasies. Sorem had turned away, was striding out of the room. Telzey watched him go, aware of Barrand's and Nelt's speculating eyes on her.

"If I'd been able to breathe," she gasped suddenly, "I'd have made more noise than that little animal!"

The beautiful COS dolls tried to smile at her.

"Their recorders couldn't distinguish whether those psi jolts came from the yoli or from me," Telzey said. "And with the racket the yoli was making, it really was more likely it was doing it."

"So the final decision still is being postponed?" Keth said.

"Only on how to go about it, of course. The other two want to know whether I'm a psi or not, what we've learned, whether we were after the Big Deal in the first place. Osselin thinks that's no longer so important. He wants to get rid of us in a way that's safe, and take his chances on everything else. He's giving Barrand and Nelt a few more hours to come up with a good enough reason against his plan—but that's the way it's to be."

Keth shook his head. "He thinks that?"

"Yes, he thinks that."

"And at the same time he's to make sure that it's *not* the way it's to be? Isn't he aware of the contradiction?"

"He's controlled," Telzey said. "He's aware of what I let him be aware. It just doesn't occur to him that there is a contradiction. I don't know how else to explain that."

"Perhaps I get the idea," Keth said.

They were in Osselin's house. Barrand and Nelt and their retinue had left shortly after the incident with Sorem and the yoli, having plans for the evening. Osselin had asked Keth and Telzey to stay on for a while.

The difference of opinion among the COS chiefs was based on the fact that Osselin was less willing to risk a subsequent investigation than his colleagues. The forcing lie detector probes Barrand and Nelt wanted would involve traceable drugs or telltale physical damage if the subjects turned out to be as intractable as he suspected these subjects might be. A gentle anesthesia quiz wasn't likely to accomplish much here. It would be necessary to get rid of the bodies afterward. And the abrupt disappearance of Keth Deboll and a companion on Fermilaur was bound to lead to rather stringent investigations even as a staged accident. Osselin intended to have them killed in a manner which could leave no doubt about the accidental manner of their death. A tragic disaster.

"What kind of disaster?" Keth asked.

"He's got engineers working on that, and it's probably already set up," Telzey said. "We'll be seen walking in good health into the ground level of our tower. Depending on the time we get there, there'll be fifty to a hundred other people around. There's an eruption of gas—equipment failure. A moment later, we're all dead together. Automatic safeguards confine the gas to that level until it can be handled, so nobody else gets hurt."

Keth grunted. "Considerate of him."

Objectively considered, it was a sound plan. The tourist tower was full of important people; various top-level cliques congregated there. There'd be then a substantial sprinkling of important victims on the ground level. Even if sabotage was suspected, nothing would suggest that Keth and Telzey had been its specific targets.

On a subterranean level of Osselin's house was a vault area, and he was in it now. They hadn't accompanied him because anyone else's body pattern would bring the vault defenses into violent action. Telzey remained in mental contact; she hadn't quite finished her work on Osselin, though there wasn't much left to do. He was sewed up as tightly as she'd ever sewed anyone up. But he remained a tough-minded individual, and she wanted to take no chances whatever tonight. Things seemed under control and moving smoothly. But she wouldn't breathe easily again until Fermilaur vanished in space behind them.

In one respect, things had gone better than they'd had any reason to expect. "Will you settle for a complete file on the Big Deal?" she'd asked Keth. "The whole inside information gathering program? The file goes back almost three years, which was when it started. Names, dates, the information they got, what they did with it. . . ."

Osselin kept duplicate copies of the file in the vault. She'd told him to bring up one copy for Keth and forget he'd had that copy then. After that, it would be a question of getting off Fermilaur—not too easy even with Osselin's cooperation. He couldn't simply escort them to a spaceport and see that they were let through. They were under COS surveillance, would be trailed again when they left the house. COS police waited at the ports. If anything began to look at all suspicious, Barrand and Nelt would hear about it at once, and act at once.

Osselin obviously was the one best qualified to find a way out of the problem, and Telzey had instructed him to work on it. He came back up from the vault presently, laid two small objects on a table, said matter-of-factly, "I have some calls to make on the other matter," and left the room again.

Keth shook his head. "He seems so normal!"

"Of course, he seems normal," Telzey said. "He feels normal. We don't want anybody to start wondering about him."

"And this is the COS file?" Keth had moved over to the table.

"That's it."

The objects were a pair of half-inch microtape cubes. Keth smiled lovingly at them, took out a card case, opened it, ran his thumbnail along a section of its inner surface. The material parted. "Shrink section," he remarked. He dropped the cubes inside, sealed the slit with the ball of his thumb. The case was flat again and he returned it to an inner pocket.

Telzey brushed her hair back from her face. The room wasn't excessively warm, but she was sweating. Unresolved tensions. . . . She swore mentally at herself. It was no time to get nervous. "How small are they now?" she asked.

"Dust motes. I get searched occasionally. You drop the whole thing into an enlarger before you open it again, or you're likely to lose whatever you've shrunk." He glanced at his watch. "How far has he got on that other matter?"

"I haven't been giving much attention to it. I'm making sure I have him completely tied up—I'll probably have to break contact with him again before we're off Fermilaur."

"You still can't control him at a distance?"

"Oh, I might. But I wouldn't want to depend on that. He seems to have the details pretty well worked out. He'll tell us when he gets back."

"The pattern will be," said Osselin, "that you've decided to go out on the resorts. What you do immediately after you leave the house doesn't matter. Live it up, mildly, here and there, but work around toward Hallain Palace, and drop in there an hour and a half from now. If you don't know the place, you'll find its coordinates on your car controls."

"I can locate Hallain Palace," Keth said. "I left money enough there five years ago."

"Tonight you're not gambling," Osselin told him. "Go to the Tourist Shop, thirteenth level, where two lamps have been purchased against Miss Amberdon's GC account."

"Lamps?" repeated Keth.

"They're simply articles of the required size. You'll go to the store's shipping level with them to make sure they're properly packaged, for transportation to Orado. They're very valuable. You'll find someone waiting for you with two shipping boxes. You'll be helped into the boxes, which will then be closed, flown directly to Port Ligrit, passed through a freight gate under my seal, and put on board an Orado packet shortly before takeoff. In space, somebody will let you out of the boxes and give you your tickets." Osselin looked at Telzey. "Miss Orm and her mother are on their way to another port, accompanied by two Hute specialists who will complete Miss Orm's modeling reversion at her home. They'll arrive at the Orado City Terminal shortly after you do. You can contact them there."

"How far can you trust him?" Keth asked, as Osselin's house moved out of sight behind their car.

"Completely now," Telzey said. "Don't worry about that part! The way we're still likely to run into trouble is to do something at the last moment that looks suspicious to our snoops."

"We'll avoid doing it then," said Keth.

Telzey withdrew from contact with Osselin. He considered the arrangements to be foolproof, providing they didn't deviate from the timetable, so they probably were foolproof. Tracer surveillance didn't extend into enclosed complexes like Hallain Palace, where entrances could be watched to pick them up again as they emerged. By the time anyone began to look through the Palace's sections for them, they'd have landed on Orado. There'd be nothing to indicate then what had happened. Osselin himself would have forgotten.

They stopped briefly at a few tourist spots, circling in toward Hallain Palace, then went on to the Palace and reached it at the scheduled time. They strolled through one of the casinos, turned toward the Tourist Shop section. At the corner of a passage, three men in the uniform of the Fermilaur police stepped out in front of them.

There was a hissing sound. Telzey blacked out.

6

Barrand said, "Oh, you'll talk, of course. You'll tell us everything we want to know. We can continue the interrogation for hours. You may lose your minds if you resist too stubbornly, and you may be physically destroyed, but we'll have the truth from both of you before it gets that far."

It wasn't the escape plan that had gone wrong. Barrand and Nelt didn't know Osselin was under Telzey's control, or that she and Keth would have been off Fermilaur in less than an hour if they hadn't been picked up. They'd simply decided to override Osselin and handle the situation in their own way, without letting him know until it was too late to do anything about it. Presumably they counted on getting the support of the COS associates when they showed that the move had produced vital information.

Their approach wasn't a good one. Telzey had been fastened to a frame used in restructuring surgery, while Keth was fastened to a chair across the room. Frame and chair were attachments of a squat lie detecting device which stood against one wall. A disinterested-looking COS surgeon and an angular female assistant sat at an instrument table beside Telzey. The surgeon had a round swelling in the center of his forehead, like a lump left by a blow. Apparently neither he nor the assistant cared to have the miracles of cosmetology applied to themselves.

They were the only two people in the room who weren't much concerned about what was going on. Telzey couldn't move her head very far and had caught only one glimpse of Nelt after she and Keth were brought awake. But Barrand remained within her range of vision, and his heavy features were sheened occasionally with a film of sweat. It was understandable. Barrand had to get results to justify his maneuver against Osselin. He might have regarded this as an opportunity to break down Osselin's prestige and following in the association. And so far Barrand could be certain of only one thing. He was, in fact, dealing with a psi.

He looked as if he almost wished he hadn't made the discovery.

From Telzey's point of view, it couldn't be avoided. Regaining contact with Osselin might be the only possible way to get them out of the situation, and she didn't know whether she could do it in time. The subtle approach was out now. While Keth, doing his part again, argued angrily and futilely with Barrand and Nelt, she'd been driving out a full-sweep search probe, sensitized to Osselin's mind patterns. Barrand's expression when he stared at her told her his psi recorder was registering the probe. So, of course, was Nelt's, whose impatiently muttering voice Telzey could hear in the section of the room behind her. He was keeping it low, but it was fairly obvious that he was hurrying along preliminary briefing instructions to the lie detector as much as he could without confusing the device or giving it insufficient information to work with. They were anxious to have it get started on her.

She hadn't picked up a trace of Osselin yet. But almost as soon as she began reaching out for him, she'd run into a storm of distress signals from another familiar mind.

It had turned into a bad day for Uspurul. Shortly after noon, she was called in to COS Services' regional office. Something happened there. She didn't know what. A period of more than an hour appeared to have lapsed unnoticed, and nobody was offering any explanations. She'd heard of amnesia treatments, but why should they have given her one? It frightened her.

She pretended that everything seemed normal, and when she was told to go to her quarters and rest for a few hours because she might be given a night assignment, she was able to convince herself that the matter was over—she'd been brushed briefly by some secret COS business, put to some use of which she was to know nothing, and restored to her normal duties.

An hour ago then, she'd been told to check out an aircar for a night flight to the Ialgeris Islands, registering Miss Amberdon and a Mr. Deboll as her passengers. That looked all right. Amberdon was still her assignment. The Ialgeris tour, though a lengthy one, requiring an expert guide because it involved sporadic weather risks, was nothing unusual. She took the car to one of the Barrand centers where she was to pick up the passengers. There she was conducted to a sublevel room and left alone behind a closed door. Misgivings awoke sharply again. There was no detectable way of opening the door from within the room.

Why should they lock her in? What was happening? Uspurul became suddenly, horribly, convinced that she'd been drawn deep into one of those dark COS activities she'd hardly even let herself think about. A fit of shaking came over her and it was some minutes then before she could control her muscles. Shortly afterward, the door opened. Uspurul stood up quickly, putting on a servile smile. The smile was wiped away by the shock of realizing that the man in the door was Nelt—one of the biggest of the COS big shots, one of the people she least wanted to see at present. Nelt beckoned her out into the passage.

Uspurul stepped out, legs beginning to shake again, glanced up the passage and felt she'd dropped into a nightmare. Barrand, the COS president, stood thirty feet away at an open door, speaking to a man in surgeon's uniform. Beside them was a float table, and on it lay two covered figures. Uspurul didn't doubt for an instant that they were those of her prospective passengers. Neither they nor she were to reach the Ialgeris Islands. Tomorrow the aircar would be reported lost in a sea storm, as a number were each year in spite of all precautions—

The surgeon moved the float table through the door, and Barrand followed it. Nelt turned away and walked along the passage toward the room, leaving Uspurul standing where she was. For a moment, hopes flickered wildly in her. She might be able to get out of the center unnoticed, find a place to hide —stay alive!

A great black-gloved hand came down on her shoulder. Uspurul made a choked screeching noise. Nelt didn't look around. He went on into the room and the door closed.

Sorem, whose black-uniformed tall figure Uspurul had seen once at a distance, Barrand's bodyguard, whose head was always covered in public by a large, disturbingly shaped helmet, unlocked the door to an adjoining room, went in with

Uspurul and shoved her down on a bench. She'd heard stories about Sorem. Half fainting, staring fascinatedly at him, she hoped he wouldn't take off the helmet.

But he did, and the yellow-eyed black dog head grinned down at her.

The lie detector was asking its patterned series of trap questions on the matters it had been instructed to investigate, and Telzey was answering them. It was nerve-stretching work. They'd stripped her before fastening her to the frame, and she'd been warned that if she refused to answer or the detector stated she wasn't telling the truth, the surgeon was ready to restructure one of her arms as a start.

She'd split her awareness again, differently, deeply. The detector's only contact was with a shadow mentality, ignorant of the split, memoryless, incapable of independent thought. A mechanism. When a question was asked, she fed the mechanism the answer she wanted it to give, along with the assurance that it was the truth. It usually was not the truth, but the mechanism believed it was. Psi sealed Telzey's mind away otherwise both from the detector's sensors and from crucial body contacts. There were no betraying physical reactions.

It took much more concentration than she liked—she'd still found no mental traces of Osselin, and a purposeful search probe absorbed concentration enough itself. But she needed time and was more likely to gain time if she kept their attention on her, away from Keth. He wasn't being questioned directly, but Telzey suspected the detector was picking up readings from him through the chair to which he was fastened and comparing them with the readings it got from her. There was a slight glassiness in Keth's look which indicated he'd gone into a self-induced trance as soon as the questions began, couldn't hear either questions or answers, hence wasn't affected by them. He'd said he could hold out against a lie detector by such means for a while. But a sophisticated detector had ways of dealing with hypnotic effects, and the COS machine obviously was an advanced model. She should keep it working away at her as long as possible.

The questions ended abrupty. Telzey drew a long, slow breath.

She might have caught a touch of Chan Osselin's mind just

then! She wasn't sure. The stress of maintaining her defense against the detector had begun to blur her sensitivity.

The lie detector's voice said. "Deboll does not respond to verbal stimuli at present. The cause can be analyzed if desired. Amberdon's response to each question registered individually as truthful. The overall question-response pattern, however, shows a slight but definite distortion."

"In other words," Barrand said from behind Telzey, "she's been lying."

"That is the probability. The truth registration on individual questions is not a machine error. It remains unexplained."

Barrand and Nelt moved into Telzey's range of vision, looked down at her. Nelt shook his head.

"I don't like that," he said uneasily.

"Nor I," said Barrand. "And we can't be sure of what else she's doing. Let's speed up the procedure! Have the detector get Deboll out of whatever state he's in and start questioning him immediately. Put on full pressure at the slightest hesitation. Take the girl off the machine for the time being." Barrand looked at the surgeon. "Get to work. To begin with, I want the left arm deboned to the wrist and extended."

The surgeon's look of disinterest vanished. He drew back the sliding top of the instrument table. "A functional tentacle?"

Berrand grunted. "She's to stay alive and able to talk. Aside from that, keep her functional if you can, but it's not of primary importance. Let her watch what's happening." He added to Telzey, "We'll stop this as soon as you demonstrate to our satisfaction that you're willing to cooperate."

All the energy she could handle was reaching for Osselin's mind now. But the trace, if it had been one, had vanished. The sculpting frame moved, bringing her down and around. The surgeon's face appeared above her. An arm of the frame rose behind him and she saw herself in the tilted mirror at its tip.

"Don't let her lose consciousness," Barrand was saying to the surgeon's assistant. "But keep the pain level high—close to tolerance."

The skin on the odd lump in the center of the surgeon's forehead quivered and drew back to either side. The lump was a large dark bulging eye. It glanced over at Telzey's face independently of the other two eyes, then appeared to align it-

self with them. Part of Telzey's mind reflected quite calmly
that a surgeon might, of course, have use for an independent
eye—say one which acted as a magnifying lens.

But this was getting too close. Barrand and the detector
weren't giving her the time she'd hoped to have.

"Chan Osselin!" She blasted the direct summons out, waited for any flicker of reaction that could guide her back to
him.

Nothing.

Uspurul had been in an entertainingly hysterical commotion
for a few minutes, but then she'd simply collapsed. Sorem
wasn't sure whether she was conscious or not. When he prod-
ded her with a finger, she made a moaning noise, but that
could have been an automatic response. Sullenly, he decided
to leave her alone. If she happened to die of fright here, it
wouldn't really matter, but Barrand would be annoyed.

Sorem stood up from the bench on which he'd been sitting,
hitched his gun belt around, looked down at the child-sized
figure sprawled limply on the floor, eyes half shut. He nudged
it with his boot. Uspurul whimpered. She still breathed, at any
rate. The black dog head yawned boredly. Sorem turned away
toward the door, wondering how long it would be before they
got what they wanted in the detector room.

Uspurul opened her eyes, looked for him, rolled up quietly
on her feet.

Sorem had good reflexes, but not abnormally good ones; he
was, after all, still quite human. And, at the moment, he was
less than alert. He heard a faint, not immediately definable
sound, felt almost simultaneously a violent jerk at his gun
belt. He whirled, quickly enough now, saw for an instant a
small face glare up at him, then saw and heard no more. The
big gun Uspurul held gripped in both hands coughed again,
but the first shot had torn the front of Sorem's skull away.

Telzey couldn't see the door opening into the lie detector
room, but she was aware of it. For an instant, nobody else in
the room was aware of it; and after that, it hardly mattered.
Sorem had fancied a hair-triggered gun, and Uspurul was
holding the trigger down as she ran toward Barrand and Nelt,
swinging the gun muzzle about in short arcs in front of her.
Most of the charges smashed into floor and wall, but quite

enough reached the two COS chiefs. Nelt, already down, moments from death, managed to drag out his own gun and fire it blindly once. The side of Uspurul's scalp was laid open, but she didn't know it. Nelt died then. Barrand already was dead. Uspurul stopped shooting.

"Deboll," the lie detector's voice announced in the room's sudden silence, "is now ready for questioning."

Telzey said softly to the surgeon, "We don't exactly need you two, you know, but you won't get hurt if you do as I tell you. She'll do whatever I want."

"She will?" the surgeon breathed. He watched Uspurul staring at him and his assistant from twelve feet away, gun pointed. They'd both frozen when the shooting started. "What are we to do?"

"Get me off this thing, of course!"

He hesitated. "I'd have to move my hands. . . ."

"Go ahead," Telzey said impatiently. "She won't shoot if that's all you're doing."

The frame released her moments later. She sat up, slid off it to the floor. Across the room, Keth cleared his throat. "You," Telzey said to the bony assistant, "get *him* unfastened! And *don't* try to get out of the room!"

"I won't," the assistant said hoarsely.

"My impression," Keth remarked some hours later, "was that we were to try to stall them until you could restore your mental contact with Osselin and bring him to the rescue."

Telzey nodded. "That's what I wanted. It would have been safest. But, like I told you, that kind of thing isn't always possible. Barrand wouldn't let me have the time. So I had to use Uspurul, which I *didn't* like to do. Something could have gone wrong very easily!"

"Well, nothing did," said Keth. "She was your last resort, eh?"

"No," Telzey said. "There were a few other things I could have done, but not immediately. I wasn't sure any of them would work, and I didn't want to wait until they were carving around on me, or doped you to start talking. Uspurul I could use at once."

"Exactly how did you use her?" Keth asked.

Telzey looked at him. He said, "Relax! It's off the record. Everything's off the record. After all, nobody's ever likely to hear from me that it wasn't the famed Deboll ingenuity that broke the biggest racket on Fermilaur!"

"All right, I'll tell you," Telzey said. "I knew Uspurul was around almost as soon as we woke up. She's very easy psi material, so I made good contact with her again, just in case, took over her mind controls and shut subjective awareness down to near zero. Sorem thought she'd fainted, which would come to the same thing. Then when I had to use her, I triggered rage, homicidal fury, which shot her full of adrenalin. She needed it—she isn't normally very strong or very fast. That gun was really almost too heavy for her to hold up."

"So you simply told her to take the gun away from Barrand's monster, shoot him and come into the next room to shoot Barrand and Nelt?" Keth said.

Telzey shook her head.

"Uspurul couldn't have done it," she said. "She'd never touched a gun in her life. Even in a frenzy like that, she couldn't use violence effectively. She wouldn't know how. She didn't know what was going on until it was over. She wasn't really there."

Keth studied her a moment. "You?"

"Me, of course," Telzey said. "I needed a body that was ready to explode into action. Uspurul supplied that. I had to handle the action."

"You know, it's odd," Keth said for a moment. "I never would have considered you a violent person."

"I'm not," Telzey said. "I've learned to use violence." She reflected. "In a way, being a psi is like being an investigative reporter. Even when you're not trying very hard, you tend to find out things people don't want you to know. Quite a few people would like to do something about Keth Deboll, wouldn't they? He might talk about the wrong thing any time. By now I've come across quite a few people who wanted to do something about me. I don't intend to let it happen."

"I wasn't blaming you," Keth said. "I'm all in favor of violence that keeps me alive."

They were on a liner, less than an hour from Orado. Once they were free, Telzey hadn't continued her efforts to contact Osselin mentally. They located a ComWeb instead, had him paged, and when he came on screen, she told him what to do. The story was that Sorem had gone berserk and killed Barrand and Nelt before being killed himself. Keth had made his own arrangements later from the liner. Adacee and various authorities would be ready to slam down on the secret COS project within a week.

Telzey's restrictions on Osselin should hold easily until then. The surgeon and his assistant had been given standard amnesia treatments to cover the evening. They could deduce from it that they'd been involved in a detector interrogation dealing with secret matters, but nothing else. It wasn't a new experience, and they weren't likely to be curious. Uspurul was aboard the liner.

"You know, I don't really have much use for a bondswoman," Keth remarked, thinking about that point.

"You won't be stuck with her contract for more than a year," Telzey said. "Keth, look. Don't you owe me something?"

He scratched his jaw. "Do I? You got us out of a mess, but I doubt I'd have been in the mess if it hadn't been for you."

"You wouldn't have had your COS story either."

Keth looked nettled.

"Don't be so sure! My own methods are reasonably effective."

"You'd have had the full story?"

"No, hardly that."

"Well, then!" Telzey said. "Uspurul's part of the story, so she can be your responsibility for a while. Fair enough? I'd take care of her myself if I didn't have my hands full."

"Why take care of her at all?"

"Because not everyone in COS is going to believe Osselin's version of what happened. They don't dare do anything about him, but there was enough to show Uspurul was involved somehow in what went on tonight. She's a rotten little creature in some ways, but I'd sooner not think of her being worked over by COS interrogation methods. They can break down amnesia treatments sometimes, so Osselin wanted to have her killed immediately to be on the safe side." Telzey added, "Uspurul's got a really good brain, and you'd be surprised at the things she's learned working for COS Services! Adacee should find her an asset. Give her half a chance, and she might make a great newscaster!"

"Adacee and I thank you," said Keth.